OPERATION: SYRIA

WILLIAM MEIKLE

SEVERED PRESS
HOBART TASMANIA

OPERATION: SYRIA

- 1 -

Corporal Wiggins laid down the law.

"This is your first time out with us. So don't fuck up. Do what I say, when I say it, and we'll get along fine. I don't expect any backchat from you new lads, is that clear?" he said and the three younger men opposite across the belly of the plane nodded.

Sergeant Hynd watched with amusement, dropped Captain Banks a wink, and went private in his headset.

"Irony is lost on that lad," the sarge said. "Maybe you shouldn't have got him that promotion, Cap."

Banks grinned.

"It hurts to say it but he deserves it, if only for his cheek," he replied. "Besides, it's not every day he'll get to enjoy being a new corporal. Let him strut for now. We'll be too busy later for any nonsense from any of them."

The plane juddered as it hit some turbulence. Banks turned to look out the window. There was only darkness beyond but he knew they must be over the mountains by now, nearing their target. Soon the red light would be switched on to signal their drop into the dark.

*

He'd been looking to ask for a period of leave for him and the squad when he was called to the colonel's office early that same morning but his superior had other ideas and Banks hardly got a chance to speak, never mind ask for a holiday.

"We need a rapid response team for a rescue mission," the colonel said with no preamble as soon as the door was closed at Banks' back. "And your squad is first up on rotation, so get kitted up. You leave inside the hour."

"We're not ready to go, sir. We're understaffed," Banks said. "What with losing Corporal McCally and not replacing those lads we lost in Antarctica yet…"

The colonel waved his objections away as if frustrated by them and interrupted.

"That's not a problem. I've already handled it. We've got five new lads in from Leuchars today. Take three of them; that'll be your choice. Find out what they're made of and if they've got the gumption to stick with it for the long haul. You know the drill."

"…and I need a new corporal," Banks finished.

"What's wrong with Wiggins?"

Banks had laughed.

Nothing much, apart from a mouth as wide and as busy as the Clyde tunnel?

He didn't say that though and the longer he thought about it, the more he knew that Private 'Wiggo' Wiggins deserved at least a chance at the post.

Having gone in expecting to get a holiday confirmed, he left the colonel's office with a new corporal, three new squaddies under his wing, and orders for a parachute drop that same night in the Syrian Desert.

*

He'd told Wiggins about the jump first.

"In the dark, onto an escarpment, in a desert? That's not much of a fucking holiday, is it, Cap? Do we at least get a camel ride out of it?"

"Aye, you're right, it's not a cushy number. But at least you'll be getting paid more for the privilege, Corporal Wiggins."

It took a couple of seconds to sink in, then Wiggins' mouth had flapped but nothing came out and Hynd laughed.

"Speechless, for once," he said.

"Nah, Sarge," Wiggins came back, his composure restored. "Just practicing my lip moves for when I next see your missus."

Wiggins' mood had improved further on being introduced to the three new lads, all privates, all on the young side and all keen as mustard.

"It won't take long for me to knock that out of them."

As for the job itself, as the colonel had said, apart from the drop in the dark it involved a rescue mission. A team of British archaeologists had got themselves caught between two rival rebel factions in the eastern Syrian Desert. An S.O.S. had come in but nothing more had been heard for the past twenty-four hours. The squad's job was to go in and see if there was anybody alive to rescue.

"At least it's not babysitting duty again," Wiggins said. "Do you think we'll see some action this time out, Cap?"

"It's Syria, what do you think?" Hynd had replied.

Knowing what he did of the area and its recent history as a hotbed of fanaticism, Banks could only agree with his sergeant. He wasn't holding out too much hope for the archaeologists.

*

When it came to choosing his three new privates, Banks went on gut instinct and chose the three who'd made eye contact with him when he called them in for a briefing. All five of the men had solid resumes—you needed to have to get seconded to the elite squads in the first place. But

3

the three who'd shown the most interest were the three he wanted on the mission. Only time would tell whether his choice was a wise one.

He had enough time for a quick briefing before leading everyone to the stores to get kitted out. As always, it was a quandary as to what to bring and what to leave but as it was a rescue mission, he went for light and fast as the default and packed only those things that wouldn't slow them down unduly. He was pleased to see that the three new men managed their own gear quickly and efficiently, then there was no more time for chat as they went out to the runway in Lossiemouth and straight onto the first of several planes.

At least they got fed and watered on the way, which wasn't always the case on these rush jobs and he'd even managed to get some sleep but now they were nearing their destination, the anticipation had his nerves thrumming as the time for the drop got close.

*

The light above him changed to blinking red, interrupting his musings. The noise in the hold went up several notches and a cold wind blew through as the rear door opened, inviting them to throw themselves out into the sky.

"Right, lads, this is it," Banks said in his headset. "Keep a tight cluster going down and maintain radio silence unless you get into trouble. If you come down and see you're alone, don't panic and don't go off on your own. We'll find you. You all know the drill."

They heaved the kit out and the team followed it out into the dark as its chute billowed open. Wiggins went first, yelling an earsplitting 'Geronimo!' Banks went last, trying to keep an eye on the others during the short freefall. Cold wind pulled roughly at his cheeks and tugged at his clothes. Ice showed for a few seconds at his goggles but quickly melted away as he descended into warmer air. He counted as he fell, pulled his cord on twenty, looked down between his feet, and was relieved to see six other chutes in a group not far below him.

There was little wind now and they descended as soft and silently as early season snowflakes. The lights of a town showed some miles to the east but he knew if he drifted that way, he was going too far off course. He took his direction from the river to his left, found the darker mound that was surely their target and followed the others down to their planned landing site half a mile farther to the west.

It had looked flat on the satellite images they'd perused at the briefing but Banks knew from painful experience that photos couldn't be trusted when it came to choosing terrain for landings, especially on a rocky desert hillside. He prepared himself for a rough landing, ready to land and drop if the need arose.

The ground came up fast out of the dark and it was more by luck than judgement that he found sound footing. He quickly got out of the harness and rolled up his chute, getting it into a tight ball before looking around for others. There was no moon but the carpet of stars overhead were enough to show him that they'd hit their proposed landing spot within a matter of yards and that all of them had got down safely. He walked quickly over to where Wiggins had got the big kit bag open.

"Rifles, handguns, helmets, radios, flashlights, small pack with field rations, spare ammo, and filled canteens," he said, keeping his voice low. "We'll stash the rest out here in case we need it later but I'm not carting full gear around if I can help it. Somebody get the wee stove and coffee though, we might get a chance of a brew."

Hynd took charge of hiding the chutes and the rest of the gear and moved off some twenty yards to the north to try to bury them. He'd only been gone a matter of seconds when he whistled, twice, from the shadows and Banks went quickly over to the sarge's position.

"I found the perfect hiding place, Cap," he said, "but somebody—something—beat us to it."

There was enough light to see that Hynd stood over a low walled well, one typical of desert areas. There was no wooden cradle holding a bucket and rope, only the circular hole in the ground. Banks leaned over but could only see blackness below, although there was an acrid odor that stung at his nose and tonsils.

"Water's off," he said.

"Aye," Hynd said. "Smells like it. But that's not what I called you over to see."

The sarge leaned forward, switched on the light on his rifle and, taking care it wouldn't be seen from a distance, shone the beam down into the depths of the well. The whole space, up to some three feet below the rim, was filled with a gray mass of fibrous string-like material that it took Banks a few seconds to identify.

"Spider web?" he said.

"Looks like it, Cap," Hynd replied. "But look at the thickness of it; yon's got to be a bloody enormous spider. And there's something else."

He moved the light over to where the web ran up the wall of the well and stopped over an area that was a lighter color, close to pure white. Banks had to lean over for a closer look before he realized he was looking at something large that had been cocooned in the web.

"What the hell is that? Goat maybe?"

"I hope so," Hynd replied. "But look again, Cap. Tell me I'm not going mad. Tell me that doesn't look like a human torso."

Banks looked again. The sarge was right and the more he looked at it, the more sure he became. There was a man wrapped up in the web down the well, wrapped up tight and stashed for later.

What the hell are we into this time?

*

Whatever it was down in the well, it wasn't an archaeologist in need of rescue, so Banks put it away, something to consider later if the need arose. His priority was on the rocky outcrop to the north, the ancient city that was the reason they were there.

He recalled what little the colonel had told him: the town was known as Dura-Europos, an important trade crossroads in ancient times, an old town even before the Romans took it for their own. It had seen numerous battles for supremacy over the trade routes then had lain undisturbed for many centuries and was a treasure trove of artifacts from half a dozen civilizations. Recently, it had become a magnet for insurgents looking for something they could loot and sell or trade for arms on international black markets. The archaeologists were here to see if anything could be rescued for posterity. Now it was they themselves that required rescuing.

Banks turned back to the squad. He didn't have the three new lads straight in his head. The tall lanky black lad was Joshua, call me Joe, Davies from Glasgow, he remembered that much, for they'd got talking over a cigarette at Munich when they switched planes and discovered they knew some people in common in the city. Of the other two, they'd both been so quiet on the trip he hadn't talked much to either. One was Brock, known to Wiggins forevermore as 'Badger' and the other was Wilkins but in their camo suits, flak jackets, and with their helmets and goggles on, in the dark, he couldn't tell them apart yet, although he thought Wilkins was the smaller, slighter lad. Not that he had much to worry about, for Wiggins was in mother-hen mode with his new charges and already had them ready to move out by the time Banks and Hynd walked back over to their position.

"All present and correct, Cap," Wiggins said. "What was so important over there?"

"Tell you later, Wiggo," Hynd said. "First job is to find somewhere else to stash the chutes."

They searched the immediate area quickly but found only rock and sand and Banks wasn't keen on using the well, knowing there was a dead man already in it. They eventually buried the chutes under a pile of rocks with the rest of their kit, leaving a new cairn on the hillside that they could only hope wouldn't attract notice until they were long gone.

Banks surveyed the terrain between them and the old walled town on the outcrop. There was a single rutted roadway leading in from the south but he ignored that; walking up and metaphorically knocking on the front door wasn't what he had in mind. To the north, close to where the edge of the town sat high on the escarpment above a long drop to the Euphrates, the outer walls had long ago tumbled into ruin. That would be their access point. It might mean some scrambling around in the dark but the rubble would also give them cover should they need it.

"Wiggo, take Davies, you've got point. I'll watch our backs. Head for the gap between the towers to the north. No shooting unless we're shot at and radio silence until we're inside. All clear?"

He got the OK sign from everybody, then allowed Wiggins to head the rest of the squad out before he followed. He had a last look backward as they walked off. He thought for a second that he saw a vaporous, oily sheen in the night hanging above the old well but when he looked again there was only the rocky hillside and the shimmering night sky above.

- 2 -

The scratching came again as Margaret "Maggie" Boyd bent over Jim White's fevered torso. Heat came off the sick man in waves and he moaned. Margaret put a hand over his mouth, trying to keep him quiet. She held her breath as the scritch-scratch outside the stone door continued for five more seconds, then fell quiet.

Silence descended once again in the chamber.

The silence of the tomb.

She had to catch the laugh that threatened to bubble up; once she started, she might not be able to stop.

Jim White's breathing slowed and he was out for the count, whether sleeping or unconscious made little difference given his condition. In their current circumstances, Maggie envied him the oblivion.

*

The attack had come without warning and so suddenly she wasn't quite sure, even two days later, what had actually happened.

And I don't know what they are.

There had been the four of them working in the fifteen-foot square chamber, digging some three feet below the old floor level: herself, Jim White, Jack Reynolds, and Kim Chung Won. The noise had come in from somewhere outside, as if funneled and amplified along the corridor. Loud shouting, then louder shooting and accompanying screams echoed loudly around them and White had been the first to react.

"Rebels," he said. "Stay here and keep quiet, I'll check it out."

The next few minutes were endless, punctuated by wails, screams, and more shooting but Maggie and the others knew better than to venture out of the chamber; it had been their choice to come to a war zone but they didn't have to be stupid about it. They could only sit, listen, and wonder as to their fate should anyone other than Jim White be the one to return.

White had come back at a run two minutes after the last shot they heard and not long after the wailing died down, leaving a silence that was nearly as terrifying. He dumped two rucksacks on the floor and turned to put his shoulder to the heavy stone doorway of the chamber.

"Help me. We need to get this closed. Get it closed now," he shouted. He was wide-eyed, pale-faced, and had blood pouring from a wound in his left shin but wouldn't speak until the door was fully shut. It took all four of them to get it into place but finally it closed with a rasp of stone on stone and sat flush with hardly a groove to show where it met the wall. Margaret had no idea how they'd ever get it open again but White didn't seem to think that a matter of import at the moment.

"Was it rebels?" Maggie asked but when he replied, it wasn't to answer the question. He looked sweaty and puffed, hair standing on end and his eyes wide and wild.

Bloody hell. What did he see out there?

"I got a message out on the radio," White said, his voice little more than a croak. "And I got us some supplies. We need to hide out here until the cavalry come for us. It's a fucking mess out there."

"Did you get a reply at the other end?" Maggie asked. "When will they get here?"

But White had spoken his last words between then and now. His eyes rolled up and he fell into a faint. They'd made him up a rough bed from the rucksacks once they'd emptied them of several bottles of water, two loaves of unleavened bread, and a bag of cheeses and meat that was all he'd managed to recover in time.

Since then, they'd settled into a routine of taking turns watching the man, sleeping and having circular conversations that could never come to any conclusions. Their only light came from two portable LED lamps they'd been using on the dig and even only using one at a time, they were visibly starting to dim. It wouldn't be long now until they would be left in the dark entirely. When that happened, the scratching was going to sound a whole lot worse.

*

The noise had started an hour after White fell into his semi-conscious state, a hard rasping as if someone stroked roughly with a stick or knife at the bottom of the door on the outside.

"Who's there?" Reynolds shouted and the rasping had turned into frantic scratching. Maggie had a cat back home in Edinburgh and it made similar sounds trying to get under the bathroom door when Maggie had the temerity to try to get some personal time in there.

I doubt that's a cat out there.

Reynolds had looked like he might call out again but Maggie shushed him with a finger to his lips.

"I don't think it's trying to get in to help us. Do you?"

Reynolds looked like that was a thought he hadn't considered and it was enough to keep his mouth shut, for now. After a few minutes, quiet had descended again.

"Rebels," Kim whispered. "It has to be. Jim said it was rebels."

"Does that sound like fucking rebels?" Reynolds replied and laughed bitterly until the scratching started again, driving them all to silence once more.

Now all they could do was wait and hope. At least they had air, which was flowing freely, a breeze coming in through a crack in the wall high up in one corner. But the bread was gone, as was the meat. All they had left was about a gallon of water and some cheese.

Even at that, White needed most of the water in an attempt to keep his fever from becoming a raging fire. The wound in his leg was suppurating, far beyond what might be expected in the time since he'd been hurt. At first, Maggie had thought it was a bullet wound but it looked more like a slashing cut from a rough-edged knife and now the lips of flesh were blackening, parting to show the flesh inside all the way down to the bone.

"We should bandage that," Kim said.

"We don't have anything clean enough," Maggie replied. "We might be doing more harm than good."

She didn't say what they were all thinking; a bandage wasn't going to conceal the fact that they shared an enclosed chamber—a cell—with a man who was likely to be dead before he took too many more breaths.

*

The scratching came every time one or the other of them so much as moved. While Kim took her turn sitting by White, Maggie sat on the lip of the dig, looking down at where they'd been working. Their excitement seemed so long ago now but at least the mosaic would be there after this was over. The chamber they were digging in had long been known to be a Roman military temple to their god Mithras but it had been thought that its treasure had all been looted. That was until the team had gone down into the floor and found the colors that had lain there hidden for centuries. So far, they'd only uncovered a quarter of it but White had hoped that it extended underfoot the whole length and width of the chamber. The bit they had uncovered so far looked complete, unbroken and protected through the centuries by the impacted sand above it. It would be a major find and as supervisor of the dig, the bulk of the credit would be going to White.

It's a pity he won't live to see it.

As if in reply to her thought, the sick man moaned loudly and that brought a fresh bout of scratching at the door.

If anybody's coming, please hurry.

- 3 -

Banks caught up with the squad at the foot of a pile of tumbled stone that had at one time been part of the town's main defensive wall. The only movement in the night was themselves, no light showed in any of the small windows and there was no sound but the soft pad and scrape of their feet on rock and sand. It was a cool night, with a slight breeze off the river and could have been any such night here for the past thousand years or more, untouched by any concerns of modernity. Banks felt like an interloper from the future as he strode up to join the others.

"Seems all clear, Cap," Wiggins said. "At least, nobody's shooting at us yet."

"Climb up and over the top, Wiggo," Banks said. "Have a shufti and let us know if it's safe to go in."

While Wiggins and Davies clambered up over the rubble, Banks and the others checked the high points for a possible ambush. But Wiggins reached the top of the rock fall without incident and waved them forward with an all-clear signal. Soon all six of them walked up through the gap in the wall to look over an internal square that had obviously been the market area of the old town in some distant past.

Now it was empty and quiet. There was no sign of life but there were numerous indications that there had been a recent firefight. Weapons fire had punched holes in walls, shell casings lay scattered around and blood, black in the night under the stars, was splashed liberally over ground, walls, doorways, and window frames. There were no bodies to be seen.

"That has to be the tidiest fucking gunfight you ever did see," Wiggins muttered in Banks' earpiece, then went quiet after being given a sharp glance. Banks sent him west along the wall with Davies, sent the sarge and Brock to the east, and motioned that Wilkins should follow him, walking slowly down the middle of the square. They found more blood, more shell casings, but nobody shot at them and nothing moved in the shadows.

After a few minutes, they reached the south end of the square, where three different exits led into a warren of high sandstone alleyways. The other four men joined them, Hynd and Wiggins both shaking their heads to indicate they'd found nothing untoward. Banks was loath to split the team up in the alleys, so he sent them all forward as one, while he once again brought up the rear.

They crisscrossed their way through the ancient town, finding nothing but darkness and dust and shadow.

*

They were making their way down another tall, empty, alleyway and Banks was beginning to think they'd been sent on a wild goose chase when Wiggins brought the squad to a halt and motioned Banks forward. Banks walked up to stand at the corporal's shoulder and looked out of the alleyway and into a courtyard beyond.

They'd found their first sign that the place wasn't completely empty, although the body that lay in the center in the courtyard was in too many pieces to be alive. Banks left Hynd with the new lads in the alleyway and walked over with Wiggins to investigate. Blood lay in three separate pools around a dismembered torso, the limbs of which looked to have been snipped off by a giant pair of scissors. One arm lay ten feet from the body but of the other arm, the legs, or the head, there was no sign. The scraps of ragged military-grade clothing and leathery skin on the torso told Banks it probably wasn't one of the archaeologists they were after but beyond that they had no more clues as to the dead man's identity. If he'd had a weapon, there was none to be found in the immediate area.

Wiggins stepped away, studying something on the ground, then motioned Banks forward. They found more blood and followed a trail of it that led across the courtyard away from them, down another alley to yet another courtyard, and into the doorway of a squat, cubic building that dominated the far quadrant. A radio set, busted as if stomped on by something heavy, lay in pieces at the side of the door, and there was more blood pooled here and more shell casings. They followed the blood trail inside, noting a spatter of droplets on the floor and a red handprint on the wall. The trail led to a narrow hallway, where they lost it in the even darker shadows.

Banks motioned Hynd to bring the others forward.

"You four watch our backs," he whispered when they were all in the doorway. "Wiggo and I will have a quick look around in here. Keep your eyes peeled. My guts are telling me there's more to this than we can see."

*

Once inside the hallway, Banks felt secure enough to turn on the light on his rifle and let it show him the path of the blood trail. It led them past two doorways that only opened into empty rooms, then stopped completely at a blank wall of stone. He was about to investigate when Hynd spoke in his ear from back at the main door.

"We've got movement on the rooftops, Cap, a lot of movement. Too dark to make out how many but I think they've got us boxed in."

16

"Could we make a run for it?"

"Tricky. They've got the high ground and would have us in a gauntlet. The good news is they're not shooting at us yet."

"Stay in the doorway. Maybe they don't know how many of us there are. Don't shoot first but keep an eye on them."

"Willco."

He turned back to see Wiggins looking at where the blood trail stopped at the wall. The corporal whispered.

"There's a wee gap here. And artificial light coming from under the bottom. I think this is a door, Cap."

Banks rapped hard on the stone in front of this face with the butt of his rifle, 'shave and a haircut.' In reply, he heard a faint yelp of surprise from somewhere beyond, then a voice, a woman, shouting as if in the distance.

"We can't get it open from this side."

Banks found the slightest of vertical cracks, marking where the supposed doorway sat in the wall but could see no lock, handles, or mechanism for getting it open. It was going to need brute force. A lot of it.

"Sarge, come in."

"Right here, Cap."

"What's the situation?"

"Still the same. There's plenty of movement on the rooftops but no clean sight. But it's not insurgents or rebels, Cap. I don't think they're people. Dogs maybe, unless there's baboons or some such in this area. Whatever they are, they don't move like men."

"Can you spare two of the lads? We've got some heavy work needing doing. We might have found some folks."

"They're on their way."

The privates, Davies and Brock, arrived alongside Banks and Wiggins seconds later. Banks made one last check of the vertical grooves that marked the door, then shouted, loudly enough that any people inside would hear.

"Stand back, we're going to give it a try."

All four of them put their shoulder against the door on the left side. Stone creaked and rasped against stone and the door moved but only by half an inch.

"Harder, lads," Banks said and put his whole weight into it. The door slid inward another inch, then something gave way and it slid faster, swinging open. Two women and a man, pale but alive, stood in a square chamber on the other side.

"Are you the cavalry?" one of the women said in a Scottish accent.

"If you're the archaeologists, aye, that'll be us. But I was told there were ten of you."

"There were," the woman said and there was a sob in her voice. She had a story to tell, that much was clear, but there wouldn't be time to hear it. Hynd came through at Banks' ear.

"Whatever they are, I think we've pissed them off, Cap. We've got incoming."

The shooting started as Banks led the other three men back to the main door.

*

He only had time to shove in his earplugs before joining Hynd and Wilkins. The two men were in kneeling position, one on either side of the doorway. Banks threw himself flat on the ground between them, leaving as little target area as possible for a sniper but it was already clear nobody was firing back and both Hynd and Wilkins had stopped shooting.

"What've we got, Sarge?" he shouted.

"Buggered if I know, Cap. We put something down as it came off the roof; it fell into the alleyway on the right and now everything's gone quiet again."

Banks turned.

"Wiggo, with me. The rest of you cover us."

Banks, with Wiggins at his shoulder, set off at a crouching run across the courtyard, then slowed as they approached the alleyway entrance. Banks switched on his gun light and aimed at a darker shadow on the ground.

It wasn't a rebel insurgent, or a dog, or a baboon, although it was large enough to have been mistaken for one in the shadows. But no baboon he knew of had red, compound eyes, a squat bulbous body or eight, stocky hairy legs. Whether it had been Hynd or Wilkins that shot it, they'd blown away a chunk of the body but it was clear enough what the thing had been. If he didn't know better, he'd have identified it as a tarantula but one of enormous proportions.

Spiders. Why does it have to be bloody spiders.

- 4 -

The archaeologists stood in the chamber, watching the open door. Silence had fallen outside after the initial volley of shots. The soldiers had arrived, then left again so suddenly that Maggie wasn't completely sure she hadn't imagined them through sheer force of hope.

"What are we supposed to do now?" Kim said. "Do we follow them?"

"It might not be safe to go out yet. I vote we close the door again, to be sure," Jack Reynolds replied.

"No," Maggie said. "Leave it be. It might have been luck they got it open the last time. I've spent enough time in this tomb as it is. I need some fresher air."

Before the others could stop her, she stepped out into the hallway. It was full dark outside the chamber but she remembered the way to the main entrance well enough to be able to feel her way along the corridor. A strange odor hung in the air, acrid, like burning plastic, stronger the closer to the entrance she got. She saw a slightly lighter patch ahead and headed for it, arriving at the doorway as two of the soldiers dragged something across the courtyard to drop it at the feet of the others.

She let of a yelp of surprise when she stepped forward and looked down at the broken remains of a spider the size of a large dog.

"What the bloody hell is that?" she said.

The man who'd spoken to her earlier looked over the top of the dead thing and smiled thinly.

"We were kind of hoping you could tell us."

*

"I'm Maggie Boyd," she said once they were back in the chamber, making the introductions.

"Are you in charge, miss?" the obvious leader of the men said.

"No, that would be Jim," she replied, pointing to the sick man on the makeshift bed. "Can you do anything for him?"

The captain—he'd introduced himself as Banks—sent the tall black private, Davies, to seeing if anything could be done about the sick man, then turned to the other men.

"See what you can do about getting these people fed and watered. Get a brew on. They look like they need it."

There was food, coffee, and a feeling of safety to be had for the first time in days. The corporal, Wiggins, left with food and drink for the three others who were on watch at the main doorway and the windows of the two rooms in the corridor outside the chamber.

"We need to get Jim to a hospital," Maggie said. "He's got a raging fever for one thing."

"I can see that," Banks replied. "But first I need to be sure you're the only four who survived. Do you know what happened to the others?"

She pointed to where Davies was working on the wounded man.

"Jim was the only one who saw anything and he didn't stay awake long enough to tell us. The rest of the team was out in the city somewhere when it went down. But we heard shots and none of us carried arms. There were definitely rebels around."

Banks nodded.

"Aye. We found one of them earlier but none of your team. If they're alive, there's a possibility they've been kidnapped for ransom. I need to call this in, see if they've heard anything back home."

21

The captain left her in the chamber to make his call. Kim and Reynolds were eating and catching up on their coffee, so Maggie went over to see if she could help Davies with the sick man.

The tall private had finished bandaging up the wounded leg. He looked grave.

"He'll lose that leg for sure," he said, his Glaswegian accent coming through strong. "It's not gangrene though, although it looks like it. Venom at a guess."

"You think it was a spider, like the one you killed?"

"If you pressed me for an answer that fits, aye, I do think that."

"But he'll live?"

Davies didn't reply at first, then said softly, "I think that's in the lap of the gods. I've given him morphine, so he should at least be comfortable for a while. But you were right, he should be in a hospital."

*

Captain Banks returned five minutes later and he too looked grave as he addressed Maggie.

"It's what I feared. There's been a video online; a group of rebel insurgents have the rest of your team held hostage. The brass doesn't know where but can only say it's somewhere within ten miles of here. And they can't risk sending a chopper in for us in case the rebels see it as provocation and kill your people."

"Surely there's something you can do?"

"There is," Banks said. "Trouble is dawn's coming up fast so we might not have enough time to search. I'm leaving two men here with you, Davis to look after your man, and Corporal Wiggins. They'll keep watch and stop anything getting to you."

"What are you going to do?"

"There's a town three miles down the riverbank that's our best bet as to where they're holding the hostages. That's where we're going. And we're going right now. If we're not back by dawn, Corporal Wiggins is in charge. Our helmet radios won't work at that range, so I've given him the sat-phone. He's a good man. If we don't make it back, he'll get you home."

- 5 -

Banks led them out, with Brock and Wilkins behind and the sarge watching their backs. His nerves had settled; now there was a definite goal in sight, although the dead spider preyed on his mind. It was the wild card on the equation, the thing he couldn't control so he compartmentalized it, put it away for later. As they left the building into the courtyard, he checked the roofs but if anything was up there, it wasn't inclined to attack and they were able to make their way back through the quiet city without any interference.

He trusted Wiggins to keep everyone in the building safe. The squad's main job now was to rescue the others. He focused all his intent on that as they trotted at double time, out of the city to the east and down a winding path that led off the escarpment. They moved quickly away from the walled city and down towards the river where the lights of a town twinkled in the distance on the south bank.

By his watch, it was three hours 'til dawn. More than half an hour of that would be spent getting down there without being seen.

That doesn't give us long to reconnoiter, get in, and get out.

But it was all the time they had, so it would have to do.

*

They stayed on the narrow track as long as they could then, as they approached the outskirts of the town, moved off twenty yards to one side and away from lighting, entering the town itself via one of the rickety wooden docks on the riverside. Given that it was the early hours of the morning, Banks didn't expect anyone to be up and about but he did expect it to feel like a town, as if there was at least someone alive. This place felt as old and dead and still as the ancient ruins upon the escarpment.

The lights are on but nobody's home.

They moved quickly away from the river and entered a long narrow roadway, tall sandstone buildings looming like a ravine on either side. He sent Hynd and Brock to the left and took the right with Wilkins.

"Watch the rooftops, mind your lines of sight, and don't wait for an order to shoot if you need to take anybody out. Remember that there are civilians here somewhere. Let's get them home."

There was enough light from the stars to show their way, but the harsh street lighting in the narrow roadway only threw the scene that met them in even sharper relief. The same gray, fibrous material they'd seen in the well on their arrival hung everywhere they looked, fashioned in intricate webs that stretched across doorways and windows and, farther along the roadway, had been spun across their path between two lampposts. Something bulbous hung there in a cocoon, too small to be an adult person but whether it was a child or a dog, Banks didn't feel like stopping for a closer look.

He noticed that Wilkins had come to a halt, unable to take his gaze from the webbing.

"Keep moving," he said softly in his headset. "Remember the mission."

Across the road, he saw Hynd and Brock making their way past the open awning of a shop that had been completely enmeshed in more of the web, a mass of fiber that ran across the whole face of the building, covering the windows even on the second story.

How many of these fuckers does it take to do that?

He wasn't sure he wanted to know the answer.

They reached the end of the road where it opened out into a wide market square beyond and he realized there had to be even more of *the fuckers* than he had imagined. The gray web blanketed everything; stalls, carts, camels, ponies, and people…a great many people, all dead. Some of the bodies were in pieces like the one they'd found up in the city, others were cocooned and wrapped up tight, hanging, suspended in web, between buildings and light fittings.

Young Wilkins threw up noisily beside the torn, dismembered body of a child. Banks put a finger to his lips for silence but in truth, he didn't blame the lad; he felt gorge rise in his own throat at the sight.

"Eyes up here, lad," he said, putting his face close to Wilkins'. "Remember we're on a rescue mission. There might be someone alive to tell us what the fuck happened here."

*

At first, that was a forlorn hope. A circumnavigation of the square found no one alive, no signs of life either in the bodies on the ground or in the suspended cocoons. Hynd drew Banks' attention to a squat building in the north corner. A military jeep was parked outside, one that had a large-caliber gun mounted on the back.

"First sign of non-civilian activity, Cap," he said. "Worth checking inside?"

Banks nodded and waved Hynd forward to investigate. The sarge motioned Banks over to join him ten seconds later, standing at the doorway of the squat building. Banks had seen Hynd stand up to some rough situations in the past but he'd rarely seen him look green around the gills.

"It's bad, Cap," the sergeant said as Banks reached him. "Maybe keep the younger lads away. It's nothing they'll want to see."

Banks walked past him and headed inside. He had thought he'd seen carnage in the square but the scene inside the building was far worse. Bodies and body parts lay strewn across the floor, tables, and bar of what had obviously been a café. A head, only the head, sat on top of an electric hob, cooked and still cooking, burned into a black ball, eyes popped and running down scorched cheeks. Banks turned off the hob and covered the head with an upturned cooking pan but he knew it was a sight and a smell that would be revisiting him in his dreams.

There had been plenty of shooting in the cramped area. The bodies mostly wore military-style clothing, webbing and flak jackets and discarded weapons. Those, along with a scattering of shell casings on the floor, told Banks they been firing at something, not only each other. He suspected more of the spider-things, whatever they might be, but the only dead present were the men who'd been doing the shooting.

The bodies all felt cold to the touch, the blood congealed, dried, and gone dark; Banks guessed, from bitter experience, that whatever had happened had gone down at least a day ago, maybe even longer. With Hynd at his side, they picked their way through pools of blood and gore, breathing shallowly through their mouths.

Banks headed for a darkened doorway at the rear. His gut instinct, honed from too many such situations over the years, told him they were in the right place, that the hostages were here somewhere. It also told him that they were too late for any rescue attempt.

The hallway at the rear of the café was lit with a flickering neon strip but was dim and dark due to the now recognizable gray web hanging in sheets from the ceiling. Banks and Hynd managed to part it carefully with the barrels of their weapons, neither of them in any hurry to get any of the stuff on their hands.

They found their hostages in a cramped room, little more than a large walk-in larder, at the rear of the property.

*

There were six bodies, packed standing upright, and all had been cocooned and wrapped like the ones hanging between the buildings outside. Hynd had to work hard using his knife to cut the web away from their faces; they didn't look like locals and further cutting revealed western T-shirts, jeans, work boots, and one passport in a jacket pocket; Tim Woods, from Chislehurst, Kent.

Banks gave up all pretense of maintaining silence.

"Sarge, take Wilkins and see if you can get that vehicle going. Send Brock in to me. We'll pile these poor buggers in the back of the jeep and get them back up the hill. The least we can do for them is see they get home."

"What about these fucking spiders, Cap?" Hynd said. "There must be dozens of the fuckers if they did all this. If so, where the fuck are they now?"

"I don't have a Scooby, Sarge," Banks said. "And as long as they stay out of our way, I don't care. Let's get back up the hill so I can call in an evac order and get us the flock out of here."

*

Banks and Brock cut the dead free from as much of the web as they were able to remove. Three of the bodies bore slashing wounds similar to the one he'd seen on the sick man earlier; the others had broken necks and bite marks at their throats so deep that their heads lolled alarmingly, making the blackened wounds gape wide. Brock looked green around the gills.

"If you're going to spew, lad, take it outside. The smell's rank enough as it is without you adding to it."

To the young private's credit, he stood his ground, helping Banks free the bodies and drag them out into the hallway outside the larder. Hynd came back a few minutes later.

"We got the jeep running, Cap. There's not much fuel in her," he said, "but she'll get us back up the hill okay."

"Let's get to it then," Banks replied. "We've left Wiggo alone with those women long enough. Knowing his patter, he'll have got at least one slap by now."

- 6 -

Jim White died sometime between four and five in the morning; no one noticed until Maggie went to check on him.

"Jim?"

His eyes were closed and he wasn't breathing, whereas the last time she'd looked his chest had been rising and falling in steady breathing. She thought him to be asleep, put under by the morphine, but when she put a hand on his ribs there was no movement and, where he'd been hot to the touch before, now he felt quite cool, chilled.

"Private Davies," she called out and the man was at her side in seconds, having heard the panic in her voice,

The lanky private worked hard on the dead man with CPR and mouth to mouth but after a few minutes, it was obvious they weren't getting him back. Davies looked up at Maggie.

"He's gone. I'm sorry."

"Aye, me too," she replied. "The poor bastard probably saved our lives taking a chance on making the radio call. And this is his reward?"

Davies put a hand on her shoulder.

"This isn't on you," he said. "It was one of those bloody spiders. If you need to hate anything, hate them."

"They're dumb beasts, doing what dumb beasts do."

"Same as it ever was," Davies replied, then looked back at the body. Black sepsis had seeped through the earlier bandaging and the smell of it rose from the body.

"Give me a hand here," he said. "We'll put him in one of the other rooms; you don't need to be looking at, or smelling, a dead man for the rest of the night."

Maggie took the legs, expecting to struggle, but White looked to have lost half his body mass in the time he'd been lying on the rucksacks. What was left of him was skeletally thin and wasted like a famine victim. It was as if they carried a bag of dried skin stuffed with wood and it held about as much semblance of life. She had tears in her eyes for the colleague she'd lost but couldn't recognize the man he had been in the dead thing in her hands. She was thankful when they reached the second room down the corridor and Davies spoke quietly.

"Thank you, miss. You can put him down now, I'll take it from here."

She returned to the chamber. Kim had her head down, sobbing, and Reynolds refused to meet her gaze. She busied herself in making three mugs of coffee and took one out to where Davies now stood at the window in the first room across the corridor. He smiled sadly.

"Thank you, miss."

"The name's Maggie," she replied. "I stopped thinking of myself as a miss a long time ago."

"And I'm Joe. I stopped thinking of myself as Joshua after a few weeks on the Easterhouse estate."

She managed a smile at that.

"Thanks for what you did for Jim."

"I wish it could have been more," he said and returned to his watch at the window as Maggie took the other two cups through to the main doorway where Corporal Wiggins stood guard. He took the mug carefully, then went to light a smoke.

"Can I have one of those?" Maggie asked on a sudden impulse.

"I didn't have you pegged as a puffer," he said.

"Five years stopped," she said, taking a light and inhaling deeply.

"But if I ever needed an excuse to start again, this is it."

"You're an Edinburgh lass, aren't you?"

"Dunbar," she replied. "And you're a Weegie, like Davies through the back."

"Guilty as charged. So what's a nice lassie like you doing in a place like this?"

She nearly laughed.

"Don't give me any of your Glesga patter," she said. "This isn't the Barrowland Ballroom and I'm not in the mood."

Wiggins laughed.

"Maybe later then," he said, then saw she was serious.

"Sorry, lass, it's just my way. How's your friend doing?"

"He's not," she said bluntly.

"Oh fuck. Then I'm really sorry," Wiggins replied, then went quiet.

Maggie looked out over the courtyard as she smoked and drank the coffee. Everything looked still and quiet, as it had when they'd first arrived.

Shit, was it only a week ago? It feels like months.

She thought for the first time in a while about the others, the six they hadn't seen since the rebel attack and wondered now whether it was rebels that had taken them, or whether it had been the same beasts that did for Jim White.

Wiggins had been silent for several minutes. She had the impression that might be something of a record for the man and was proved right when he spoke up again.

"So what's the deal with these big fucking spiders?" Wiggins asked.

"Sorry, no idea. That one you shot was the first we'd seen of them. If it was them that got Jim White, we didn't see it."

She looked out the doorway again; somebody had moved the spider carcass outside and off to one side. It lay in the shadows, a broken thing, all twisted legs and strangely deflated body.

"Spiders don't grow that big," she said.

Wiggins laughed.

"I guess they do now."

"No, I mean they can't grow that big. The circulatory and respiratory systems aren't built for it. Once they get past a certain size, about the size of your hand, they can't get enough oxygen inside them fast enough to drive their functions."

Wiggins laughed again.

"That one was coming for us fast enough. And the shadows on the roofs are faster again. They're still up there, watching us right now I'll bet. I don't think they know they have a problem."

"I don't understand anything that's going on here."

"Don't let it bother you," Wiggins replied. "It happens to me all the time."

*

When she returned to the chamber, Kim was down in the trench, working on the mosaic with a soft brush and a trowel.

"There's not enough light for that kind of work," Maggie said.

"I tried to tell her," Jack Reynolds replied dully, "but she's not talking. Leave her be; she needs something to take her mind off the rest of this shit."

"I know how she feels."

Maggie sat on the floor, watching Kim scrape layers of dry dirt from the mosaic. Reynolds was first to break the silence.

"That corporal at the door...he's got the sat-phone, hasn't he? Did you persuade him to make the call, to get us the fuck out of here?"

"He's waiting for the others to come back."

"If they ever come back. This is fucked up. We should never have come here."

"We're archaeologists. It's our job to save this kind of thing."

"Sure. But nobody told me I'd have to be Indiana Fucking Jones as well."

Kim hadn't spoken but was now working faster, furiously, sweeping dirt aside from directly over the mosaic. Maggie looked down. She'd already cleared a large patch, depicting Roman centurions both on foot and in chariots, all with weapons facing inwards to a central point in the design. The central area was now under Kim's brush as she swept and cleared ever more frantically.

Maggie stood and fetched a light, taking it over to see more clearly but Kim was bent over, brushing, obscuring the two-foot circle that was the central motif as it was finally fully revealed. It was only when Kim sat back and let out a long gasp that became a wail when they saw what was there.

A fat dark spider lay directly in the middle of the mosaic, surrounded by Romans stabbing at it or spearing it with lances. Dead men lay under its legs, which spread far out into the mosaic itself. Maggie now realized that the whole thing was cunningly depicted as a single huge web. The face of the spider was the worst thing. It smiled, an evil grin under compound eyes as it sucked the life from a man it held in its mouth. The man was dwarfed by the bulk of the body, which, if the proportions of the thing were to be believed, was at least ten feet from head to rear.

-7-

It was a tight squeeze to get everybody and the bodies into and onto the jeep. When Banks sat in front beside Wilkins, the nominated driver, the sarge and Brock were, somewhat precariously, perched in the back beside the gun, with the dead stuffed, haphazardly and with little in the way of respect, on the floor at their feet. It didn't help that they were partially encased in web, or that the black wounds were suppurating, an advanced decay having set in that stank even worse than the cooked head on the hob had done.

The only good thing about the situation was that Brock had found a belt of ammo for the big gun and had loaded it up; if anyone came at them, they were going to get a blast of high-caliber shells in their face as introduction.

The main road out of the square was the one they needed to take to head back up to the escarpment and the ancient town on the hill. Banks kept an eye on the rooftops, fearing an ambush as Wilkins drove them away.

"We're not stopping for anyone or anything, got that, lad?" he said.

"Got it, sir," Wilkins replied. He handled the jeep like someone used to driving fast. He put his foot down hard as they left the square and they sped through the empty town leaving a cloud of dust and sand in their wake. Banks checked his wing mirror and saw that the sky was lightening in the east at their back.

Dawn was coming.

*

The rest of the town looked as dead—murdered—as the part they'd left. Gray web cloaked many of the shops and dwellings and more cocooned bodies hung from balconies and light fittings, swaying in the breeze. Some of them oozed, dripping black noxious fluids and again Banks glimpsed a wavering, oily vapor in the air, one that he thought might be luminescent in full dark. He was glad of the approaching sunrise as they barreled through the empty streets.

It was going too well to last. They approached the edge of town and could clearly see the road winding upwards towards the escarpment but the way ahead was blocked the full stretch across by a mass of web, thick enough to be nearly solid. It was also eight feet high and definitely impassable.

"Sir?" Wilkins said. "What do you want to do?"

Banks considered telling the lad to put his foot down, try to blast through but the risk of getting tangled up in that gray shit was too large to take.

"Hang a left," he said. "Let's see if we can go round it."

A left turn, taken at speed, brought them into a narrow alleyway, fifteen feet high, where the night held off the approach of dawn. Wilkins put on the jeep's headlights, which showed another gray mass blocking their exit fifty yards ahead.

It's the perfect spot for an ambush.

"Back up. Back up now," Banks shouted.

It took the lad a few seconds to brake, then find reverse gear on the unfamiliar stick, and that was long enough for Banks to look in his mirror and see two of the dog-sized spiders already spinning web side to side across the alley entrance behind them.

*

"Contact rear!" Banks shouted and felt the jeep rock as Hynd and Brock tried to get the mounted gun turned to the alley entrance. Wilkins had the vehicle reversing, slowly back towards the fast-growing web. Above them black shapes loomed, darker humped shadows on the rooftops against the lightening sky.

"Bugger this for a lark," Banks said. "Floor it, lad. If we don't get through now, we never will."

The jeep shuddered as the gun in the back fired five quick blasts. The sound was deafening inside, setting Banks' ears ringing. He tried to check his mirror but all he saw was a gray blur, coming up fast. He braced his feet in the stairwell, anticipating impact but the jeep's momentum was enough to drive through the strands of web, although they were slowed considerably in the process. The big gun fired, twice more and the sarge shouted from the back, his voice coming to Banks as if from far away, in a wind.

"Incoming to the east. Multiple bogeys."

Banks wound down his window and looked out. Dawn was close now, a pinkish glow lighting the horizon. It only served to illuminate the roadway back into the town center, from where a mass of the huge spiders some thirty feet deep filled the road from side to side, scuttling as fast as a running dog, coming straight at them.

"Get us the fuck out of here, Private," Banks shouted.

Wilkins didn't pause to question the order. He swung the jeep around until they faced across the road, then floored the accelerator as they barreled into an even narrower alleyway, one just about wide enough to accommodate them. Banks' wing mirror screeched against the wall for a second then ripped off to tumble away behind them. Up top the heavy gun rattled, shaking the frame of the jeep. Ahead of them, the river was coming up fast at the end of the alley and Banks didn't see anywhere they could turn to get back to the main roadways.

Three black shadows dropped from the rooftops at the far end of the alley and immediately spun web across their exit. He had a matter of seconds to make a decision and there were no exits on either side of them, not even a doorway or window, only a blank expanse of wall looming over them.

"Floor it," he shouted and braced himself again.

*

The spiders had managed to spin half a dozen lengths of web across the entrance. The jeep went through them, barely pausing this time. Wilkins hit the brakes as they flew out the alley onto a wooden wharf but their momentum was too great. They skidded in a squeal of brakes and tires on wood, then toppled in slow-mo, off the end of the jetty. Banks felt a split second of weightlessness as they dropped four feet or so into the water, hitting the river with a hard smack.

"Bale out," Banks shouted and, having to push against the weight of water struggled out of his door as the jeep sank. He managed to stand up, thigh deep, holding his weapon high. He saw Brock trying to save the bodies in the back as the jeep drifted slowly downstream in the current.

"Leave them, lad. At least they'll get a clean burial here."

The bodies drifted away, overtaking the jeep and heading away downstream. The vehicle stuck fast as it hit bottom. The sarge stood up on the back. He trained the big gun back to the shore, where half a dozen spiders stood, front legs raised, twitching as if tasting the air.

"Have some of this, wankers," he shouted and emptied what was left of the belt of ammo into the beasts on the jetty, blasting them into pieces of leg, body, mouth parts, and burst eyes that fell into the water and drifted slowly away alongside the dead bodies.

The gun ran dry, the ringing echo of its boom and roar lasting long in Banks' ears before a silence fell again around them. All that was left on the jetty was scattered remains of blasted spiders. They waited to see if anything else was going to come out of the alleyway but it stayed shadowy and still.

With the sun rising at their backs, Banks led the men away, wading up river, staying in the water until they were well past the outskirts of the town.

- 8 -

Maggie was at the doorway with more coffee and another of Wiggins' smokes when they heard, distant but immediately recognizable, the rat-tat of gunfire, which came sporadically for several minutes before falling quiet. She saw the look that passed over Wiggins' face.

"Trouble?" she asked.

"It wasn't one of ours, that's for sure. That sounded like a bloody cannon."

"Rebels?

"Possibly. But I'm not leaving you to go and have a look, so keep your knickers on, lass."

"And any more talk like that, you'll be counting your teeth in your hands the next time," she said and smiled to show that she meant it.

Wiggins smiled back.

"Glad I know where I stand. Could you go and tell your people not to worry? They might have heard. Keep them calm. The cap and the lads will be back soon. The sun's coming up."

She looked out over the courtyard to see light in the sky through between the houses lining the east-side alleyway. It also meant she had a closer look at the dead spider than she'd wanted.

"There's something you should know first," she said and told him about the mosaic and the spider depicted in the center.

"Fucking hell," Wiggins replied when she was done. "And it's authentic, this mosaic of yours? Not a modern hoax?"

"Nope, totally kosher," she replied. "Yon spiders aren't anything new around these parts."

"You'd think somebody might have mentioned them, somewhere along the line?"

"Aye, you would. I'm guessing they've been keeping away from people, wherever they've been. And to answer your next question before you ask it, no, I don't know why they're here now. Maybe the rebels found them, disturbed them, got them riled up. But I don't know for sure."

"I don't even want to know," Wiggins said, looking out over the courtyard.

Maggie saw the worry in his face.

"They'll be back soon," he whispered.

"And if they're not?"

"I'm not even going to think about that for an hour or so yet," he replied. "But if it comes to it, I'll call in a ride to get you out of here and Davies and I will go and fetch our pals."

"I hope it doesn't come to that."

"Me too, lass. Me too."

*

When Maggie returned to the chamber, Kim was on her knees in the dig and had now uncovered two-thirds of the mosaic. There was nothing new to see that was as startling as the initial reveal of the huge spider in the center but there was one thing that hadn't been noticeable before. In the upper right quadrant of the mosaic there were other spiders, equally as large as the one in the center, depicted as emerging from a cave in a hillside. The contours of the hill were immediately familiar; it was the same escarpment they were on now, down to a detailed depiction of the old city on the skyline.

When she pointed it out to Jack Reynolds, she quickly discovered he'd lost interest in the archaeology.

"So what?" he said. "Does it help? Does it get us closer to home?"

"It's why we're here."

"Not anymore it isn't. Did your boyfriend at the door make the call? Are we getting the fuck out of here any time soon?"

"He's still waiting for the others to come back."

"Yeah? It'll be a fucking long wait if that shooting was any indication. Yes, I heard it, loud and clear. If the bloody rebels don't get to us, then we've only got the fucking spiders to worry about."

"They seem to be keeping their distance. Killing one of them seems to have given them pause."

"Pause? They're fucking spiders. Don't credit them with any kind of critical thinking. We're rats in a trap in here. They'll get in. We've all seen the movies. They always get in."

"This is real life," Maggie said. "This isn't a movie."

"Are you sure? Because it feels exactly like a fucking monster movie to me."

The conversation ended there as Reynolds went to sit against the wall, staring blankly into space. Kim wasn't speaking either, fully intent on her work with brush and trowel. Maggie envied her the focus, wishing that she had something to keep her mind off poor Jim White, or the impossible dead spider in the courtyard outside.

To make matters worse, she realized she wanted another cigarette. She busied herself in making another pot of coffee, although it had been only half an hour since the last. She never drank any of it, for as she was about to pour she heard a loud curse out in the corridor, then the building echoed with the roar of gunfire.

*

She headed for the doorway, only realizing when she exited into the corridor that she didn't have any idea what she might be able to do to help. The shooting was coming from the room opposite, accompanied by some creative swearing.

"Is that all you've got, fuckers?"

She looked in and saw Davies at the window, firing out into the street beyond. He let off three more quick shots, then stopped and shouted.

"Watch your three o' clock, Corporal. They're headed your way."

More shots, slightly muffled, came from the front at the main door. Davies turned to look at Maggie, then his gaze went over her shoulder to the chamber beyond.

"Hey, give that a rest."

She turned to see Reynolds pushing the chamber door closed from the inside, his neck muscles straining with the effort.

Wiggins stopped shooting at the front doorway long enough to shout out.

"Incoming. Multiple bogeys."

Davies looked to be in two minds, which gave Reynolds enough time to finish what he'd started. The door swung, closing faster. Davies finally stepped forward but was too late to stop it. The last thing Maggie saw was Reynolds' grim smile before stone rasped loudly against stone and the door shut firm in her face.

- 9 -

By the time Banks and the three other men reached the heights of the escarpment, they were sweating hard in their suits. Any dampness from their soaking on the river had already dried off in the rising heat of the sun during the thirty minutes it had taken them to reach the old city.

He'd kept them in the river long enough to get well clear of the town and to ensure that none of the spiders were following them along the bank. Once on dry land, he'd run them hard up the hill, both to doubly ensure escape from any pursuit from below and in worry at what might be happening to Wiggins and the rest back inside the walled town above. Despite checking over their shoulders every few steps, they'd seen no sign of any more of the spiders; they'd got free and clear on that front. But as they approached the town walls, they heard the familiar sound of weapons fire from somewhere in the warren of high alleyways of the old city.

Banks tried his headset radio.

"Wiggo? Come in?"

He heard only static in response. If it was Wiggins doing the shooting, he wasn't going to hear much of anything above the sound of his weapon.

"Double time, lads," Banks shouted and led the squad forward.

*

They were stopped in the first alley by a wall of gray web that reached from ground to rooftops some twenty feet above.

Hynd tried hacking at it with his knife but it was inches, perhaps feet, thick; an impenetrable wall. The sarge wiped the knife on his trouser leg, leaving a thick gray smear.

"No way through this way. It stinks like shite too, Cap, so don't get any on you."

They retreated away, quickly found a second route in another alley but found it too blocked to any access. The sound of gunfire intensified, a second shooter joining the first.

Something doesn't want us to see what's going on inside.

Banks tried to part the web with the barrel of his rifle but succeeded only in embedding the last inch of the barrel in the sticky fibers, needing all his strength to recover the weapon. Hynd had more luck this time with his knife—this web wasn't as thick or deep as the last one and he successfully cut a long slit vertically that could be widened with two of them carefully using their rifles to hold the lips of the slice apart. Banks slipped through first, taking care not to get tangled, then turned to do his bit holding the cut web open for the others to come through.

Wilkins was the last through but before he made it a shadow fell on them, cast by movement on the rooftop above. Two spiders, each as big as a large dog, fat bodied and with red-eyes fixed on the four men, descended fast over the parapet and scurried down the walls with a scrape of hooked talons on stone.

Banks and Hynd took out the closer of the two with a volley of three shots each. Their target fell, twitching, at their feet and Hynd buried his boot right over its red eyes, grinding it into the sand. They turned their attention upward but they were too late to get the second. It stopped scrambling and dropped, a dead weight, to land on top of Brock. The private tumbled and rolled in an attempt to get out of the way but was immediately caught in a new thread of web from the spider's rear end that tangled his hands around the rifle. Chattering, clacking black fangs, each as long as an index finger reached for his face.

"Get this fucker off me," Brock screamed.

Banks stepped forward and put his weapon at the beast's eye, making sure he wasn't going to hit Brock before putting three shots into it. The front of the beast blew apart in gore and tissue but the legs kept kicking and it continued to weave web around Brock's arms before Banks and Hynd kicked it aside and put three more rounds into it to keep it quiet.

Brock rolled and tugged but his arms were completely encased in gray fiber.

"Lie still, lad," Banks said. "You're making it worse. Let the sarge get at it."

Hynd had to use his knife again to try to free Brock, while Banks turned to Wilkins. The lad had tried to get his gun up to help in the fight and in the process had become completely tangled in the web that ran across the alley. His whole left side, from shoulder down to knee, was encased in a thick mass of the webbing. Like Brock, his frantic struggles to free himself were only making matters worse.

"You too. Stand still, lad," Banks barked. "That's a bloody order."

He had to lower his rifle to get out his knife and with Hynd likewise busy untangling Brock, they had nobody covering them. Banks' back felt too exposed as he worked at the web, having to put all his strength into the cuts and slices. He left large patches of web attached to Wilkins' clothing and gear and it stank like wet shite but he was more concerned with getting the lad free quickly than with doing an aesthetically pleasing job of it.

He was cutting, having only managed to free Wilkins' left arm when the lad looked up and all color drained from his face.

"Sir, I think we're in trouble."

Banks followed his gaze. Spiders, at least a dozen of them, lined the rooftops on both sides of the alley.

*

"Sarge," Banks said, glancing down. "You about done with Brock?"

"Five seconds, Cap, on the last strand."

He turned back and looked Wilkins in the eye. He spoke as he cut.

"No sudden movements now, son," he said. "I reckon it'll take another minute to get you out of there. So calmly does it. No shooting unless they start to come at us. Give me some warning if they make a move."

He went back to cutting, working faster now.

"Clear," the sarge said below him. "We've got your back, Cap."

Hynd stood away from Brock to allow the younger man to roll to his feet. The movement stirred the spiders into action and two of them leaned over the edge of the parapet, the clicking of their fangs sending a rat-a-tat echo along the alley.

"You need a hand with that, Cap?" Hynd said.

"Nearly done. Keep us covered. Don't wait for an order, shoot the fuckers if they move."

His gloves were covered in web that felt like heavy-duty glue under his fingers, it stank to high heaven, and the knife was being blunted with the work, less efficient with every cut and slice. He was down to Wilkins' knees and had to kneel on the ground to get at the last piece holding the youth in place.

He got lucky and was in the right place at the right time to see, dimly through the gauze of the web, more spiders advancing towards them from the far end behind Wilkins' back. It had gone quieter now; the shooting deeper in the town had stopped and the only sound to break the

47

silence was the rat-a-tat clicking of the spider's communication. It was getting more rapid, more frenzied. An attack would come at any time.

He was cutting at the web at Wilkins' knee when the shooting began; he didn't know whether Brock or Hynd fired first but it hardly mattered. The alleyway filled with the roar of weapons fire and pieces of spider legs, bodies, and a slimy, foul-smelling gore fell in rain around them. Above Banks' head, Wilkins had enough freedom to train his own gun up toward the roofs and joined the action, adding another thunderous roar of fire to the chaos.

Behind Wilkins, beyond the web, the alley filled with more spiders, a black mass of them scuttling quickly forward. Banks cut the younger man's knee free of the web as the first of the attackers reached the web and, using its fangs as scissors, began cutting its way through.

"Time to go," Banks shouted and, knowing they'd follow him, set off at pace along the alley, firing as he moved at spiders which were now coming over the lip above and making their way down the walls in a black wave.

He had to slow long enough to discard his gloves; the web had made them too sticky to be of any use. Hynd overtook him and took point. Banks let the two younger men pass and looked back. The spiders had made short work of their web and now filled the alleyway behind them, coming on fast, even while more dropped to join them from above.

*

He'd taken too long to get his gloves off and the others had moved some five yards ahead of him. A spider, even larger than the others, dropped from the rooftops and fell into the gap between Banks and the others. It made directly for him, on him before he could get a shot in. He managed to put two in its body but it didn't slow, barreling onto him and knocking him off his feet. He remembered how Brock's hands had been taken out of commission and realizing he couldn't get into position to take another shot, dropped his rifle by his side, reaching for his knife as the twin black fangs lunged for his throat. He threw his weight against the spider and was surprised to find it weighed very little. He easily rolled the thing over and stabbed again and again into the widest part of its belly while dripping wet fangs chattered and clacked right in front of his eyes. If he shifted his weight, even for a second, it would tear his face off. He stabbed and tore with the knife, feeling fluid run over his hand and wrist, a new acrid stench threatening to assault his throat and nose. Finally, the thing fell still.

He rolled away from it, retrieving his rifle in the same movement and rose, breaking into a run when he saw that the pursuing mass of spiders was only yards from catching him.

Farther up the alley the other three men were standing, back to back, sending volleys up to the rooftops. They too were covered in dripping gore and stood amid a growing pile of twitching spider bodies but they had cleared most of the beasts from above by the time Banks caught them.

"Try to keep up, Cap," Hynd said as they ceased fire. "I thought we'd lost you there."

Banks took the lead as they headed off at speed down the alley. The attack from above had been nullified but the swarm at their backs was coming on fast.

We need to get out of this alley. We're sitting ducks in here.

He upped the pace until they were full-out running. The end of the alleyway was in sight twenty yards ahead and he kept his eyes on the gap, trying not to think about the beasts at their back.

Almost clear.

A spider as large as a small car scuttled across the open end of the alleyway, totally blocking their escape route. Its rat-a-tat clacking was answered from behind them and from the rooftops in front of the running men, as a score and more of the black-bodied beasts crept over the parapets.

We're trapped.

- 10 -

Maggie stood in the hallway, fingers plugging her ears as both Davies in the room across from her and Wiggins at the main doorway along the corridor fired volley after volley out into the street. It felt like an age until the shooting stopped and even when she took her fingers out of her ears, the echo of the gunfire rang in her head. She stepped forward to see Davies load another magazine in his rifle.

"Is it over?"

"Well, they've buggered off for now, if that's what you mean," the lanky man said. "I can't see them anymore. Maybe the corporal knows more."

Davies stayed at his post as Maggie went out along the corridor again to the front of the building and the main doorway. Wiggins was likewise reloading. She looked out to see a dozen or more of the spiders lying in scattered pieces and gore in the courtyard.

"Is it over?" she asked.

"For now, I think so. But I don't understand it. There were at least fifty of the fuckers and they had us bang to rights," Wiggins said. "I was getting ready to retreat back to you and the lad for a last stand, when they all buggered off."

Before Maggie could reply, more gunshots echoed across the old town, coming from somewhere to the north, several weapons firing at once.

"Now, that's our lads and they're in trouble," Wiggins replied.

He tried his radio.

"Cap? Come in?"

All he heard in answer was more gunfire.

"Stay here," he said.

"Bugger that for a game of soldiers, Corporal," she replied. "Do you have a handgun?"

Wiggins grinned.

"I knew we were compatible," he replied and took a pistol from his hip, handing it over to her. "Safety's off. Point and shoot and keep shooting until the fuckers go away."

"Sounds like a plan to me," she said and followed Wiggins as he set off at a run across the square in the direction of the gunfire.

*

They didn't have to run far, only across the courtyard and along one alleyway to a smaller yard. It contained the mangled torso of a dead man on the ground and a huge spider, one much larger than the others, facing away from them and blocking the mouth of the route north. Gunfire came from beyond the beast and looking up, Maggie saw a wave of the smaller spiders coming down from the rooftops.

Wiggins took in the situation immediately and didn't hesitate. He fired three quick rounds into the large beast's rear.

"Three up the arse. How'd you like that, wanker?"

The spider's back end crumpled, its rear legs giving way beneath it. But the front was working well enough and it turned at Wiggins' attack and scuttled forward. Wiggins put three more rounds into its eyes and Maggie fired twice into its body. At the same time, four men came at a run out of the alleyway, all firing into the bulk of the spider which finally collapsed in a heap in the small courtyard, oozing fluids from multiple wounds.

There was no time for warm welcomes. The smaller spiders

swarmed in the alleyway from which the four men had emerged. The squad lined up in the alley mouth and send wave after wave of shots into the squirming mass of legs and bodies, blowing limbs, eyes, fangs, and bodies apart in a spray of viscous gore that smelled as bad as it looked.

It took less than a minute before nothing was left alive in the tight alley. Maggie looked up to see a dozen more spiders on the parapet but these were already slinking away across the rooftops to the north, seemingly having lost their appetite for a fight.

"Is that all of these fuckers?" Wiggins said.

*

Once they were safely back in the main doorway, the captain set Brock and Wilkins on guard duty and led her into the empty room beyond where Davies was on watch.

"I wanted to do this quietly and tell you before the others, as you're the only one that looks strong enough to take it right now," Banks said.

Maggie knew from the look in his eyes it wasn't good news and couldn't bring herself to ask, so let him continue.

"We found the rest of your team down in the town. I'm not sure what got them first but it was the spiders that got them in the end."

It was too much information to take in at once.

"They're dead? All of them?"

Banks only nodded.

"And the bodies?"

Banks told her the story, from the soldiers' entry into the town downstream, to their narrow escape on the waterfront. She was left with the one vivid image in her mind, the cocooned corpses floating serenely away down the great river where so many had gone before them in aeons past. She wanted to say something, maybe to thank the man for his efforts, but nothing would come. Banks took note and patted her softly on the shoulder, the only comfort he could offer.

"And now I need coffee and a smoke," the captain finished.

He turned away from her and only then noticed that the door to the chamber was firmly closed against them. Maggie finally found her voice.

"Reynolds and Kim are in there," she said. "Jack took fright and locked them in. We haven't had a moment to try to open it up again."

"Aye, well we've got one now." He shouted along the corridor. "Wiggo, Sarge, get your arses through here."

In the end, they needed Maggie to put her shoulder to the door alongside them but slowly, creaking rasping millimeter at a time, the door eventually swung inward.

Maggie noticed two things immediately; the crack in the upper corner where the breeze had come in was now a gaping hole three feet wide. A gray, wispy gauze of fresh webbing covered the area, like a frosted pane of thick glass. The webbing had a scrap of material in it, a piece of Reynolds' flannel shirt, red with fresh blood showing against the gray. Kim sat in the far corner of the chamber, as if trying to press herself as small and tight as possible, hands over her head as she sobbed uncontrollably. There was no sign of Reynolds save the scrap of shirt but it didn't take many smarts to figure out what had happened to him.

Wiggins stepped up to the new hole and prodded it with his rifle.

"It's not thick," he said. "We can cut through, if you need to, Cap?"

Banks looked grim.

"I don't need to. We're not going chasing around after lost lambs. Not when there are more predators about. He brought this on himself, the stupid wanker."

Maggie didn't say anything but found she was in agreement with the captain, at least on that point.

*

Banks had his men move everything out of the chamber; food, lights, rucksacks, camp stove, and Kim and the squad pulled the door shut as much as they could manage from out in the corridor. They set up a new temporary camp in the main hallway by the front entrance while Banks went through to the quiet empty room along the corridor to call the situation in to his H.Q. The sergeant, Hynd, set to making coffee while Maggie and Wiggins tried to pry Kim out of what looked like catatonic shock.

"Please, tell me what happened?" Maggie kept saying, softly but Kim had retreated somewhere unreachable and sat in a corner, balled up tight. Her eyes stared straight ahead, gazing in horror at something only she could see.

After a futile five minutes with no other information forthcoming, Maggie joined Wiggins and Hynd in a smoke with a mug of coffee.

"How's your pal?" Wiggins said.

"She's stopped crying. That's a start. But whatever she saw, it's scared her, bad."

"Aye," Wiggins replied. "I'm not too happy about it myself. I fucking hate spiders."

She was starting to get the soldiers clear as individuals in her head now, all apart from the two younger privates, who, as yet, were merged into one fresh-faced, barely out of their teens, quiet blandness. Private Davies she had spoken to, he was the tall black lad from Glasgow. The corporal, Wiggins, was a cheeky, chatty bundle of nervous energy, a cigarette smoking machine, also from Glasgow but with a harder edge, a sense of violence always present under the smile. She didn't feel uncomfortable in his presence, for she recognized the type; she'd spent long enough fending them off at university discos in her youth. Hynd was different again, maybe ten years older, the experience sitting easy on him. If Wiggins was a flighty sparrow, the sergeant was an owl, a calm center that saw everything around him, a coiled spring ready to unleash but yet content to stay still and ready for as long as it took.

The captain, on the other hand, to continue the bird analogy, would be an eagle, above everything else, looking down in search of trouble or opportunity and ready for either. She smiled at her own fancy and was smiling when Banks arrived at the doorway.

"How are you holding up?" he asked.

It was a question she'd been asking herself. There was only Kim and her left now, two out of the large team that had set off from London last week so full of excitement as to what they might find. She'd had dreams of academic success, maybe even of finds to make a career from. Now all she wanted to do was get out of here in one piece.

"I'll survive," she said in reply to Banks' question. "You need somebody to take home with you."

Banks gave her a thin smile.

"Aye, this is a fucked up trip all 'round. But it'll be over soon. There's a chopper waiting across the river that we can call on this evening as soon as it gets dark." He checked his watch. "Nine hours or so. We hunker down here 'til dusk, then they'll pick us up somewhere in the open. You'll be home before you know it."

"If the spiders let us go."

He smiled thinly.

"One way or another, we're going," he said. "We'll kill every bloody one of them if we have to and trample on what's left."

-11-

Banks took his sergeant out along the hallway to the main doorway for a smoke and brought him up to speed with the news of the proposed rescue.

"Nine hours? That's a long time to spend waiting," Hynd said. "We could sweep the area, clean out these fucking things completely?"

"We don't have enough ammo," Banks replied. "Not if there's even more of them hiding somewhere."

"Spiders as big as horses? It's not fucking natural, Cap."

"Tell me about it. But it's about par for the course for us these days. Maybe Wiggo is right. Maybe we are fucking monster magnets."

Hynd patted his rifle.

"These ones seem to go down quickly enough though, so there's that to be grateful for."

"Aye, speaking of that, take an inventory. We did a shitload of shooting out there today. See if anybody's running low and make sure everybody's got a full mag. I aim to lie low and not look for trouble but I said that earlier too and look where that got us."

He turned to the two younger men at either side of the doorway.

"I bet you're glad you got transferred to the squad now, eh, lads?"

Wilkins grinned.

"It's not every day I get cut free from a giant spider web, is it? That story should be worth a few pints back in the mess if nothing else."

Brock too grinned.

"I wouldn't want to be anywhere else, sir. Well, maybe down the pub with fitba on the telly but apart from that..."

Spirits were as high as could be expected. Banks wished his gut would settle; it was grumbling at him again, although he knew even without his early warning system that more trouble wasn't too far off.

*

Back in the hallway, Wiggins was passing out ration packs and Banks' stomach stopped growling for long enough to get something hot besides coffee inside him, although it was spoiled somewhat by the lingering stench of the gore he'd got on his hands and wrists while stabbing the spider. He'd tried washing it off with bottled water but it was ingrained deep. So he took another smoke when Wiggins offered; at least the harshness of the cheap tobacco did much to mask the smell.

The woman, Maggie, knelt on the floor again beside the quiet one, Kim, who wasn't talking. Banks wasn't sure she'd be able to tell them more than they'd already guessed; a huge fucking spider got in and carried the missing man off. When Banks had called in to the colonel back home, he'd asked for permission to go out into the city and look for the man but his superior had been adamant.

"You're to stay where you are, Captain. We can't lose anybody else. Understand?"

He'd understood more than enough. As a rescue mission, they weren't doing well and the colonel needed a win to sell to the top brass on their return. Banks main job now was to make sure he got the two women and his squad, home safe. Everything else was secondary to that.

What he hadn't told anyone yet and what had him worried, was that the chopper would need a largish open area to come down in. The market square they'd come through on their way in was the obvious spot but if the spiders were intent on controlling the town, as appeared to be the case, then getting to the spot might not be easy.

It might not even be possible.

Standing at the doorway looking out over the mangled, shot-up remains of giant spiders wasn't helping him clear his thoughts enough to come up with a solution. He went back inside to see how the sarge was getting on with the inventory.

*

"It's not great news, Cap," Hynd said when Banks found him checking on Davies. "We've hardly got a mag each left for the rifles. We've got the handguns of course but I doubt if they've got the stopping power if one of the big fuckers comes along."

"Let's hope we gave them enough to think about earlier and they leave us alone," Banks replied.

"We'll need a plan B if they do come, that's for sure. We've got five minutes of firefight left in us; after that, we're toast."

"We need somewhere they can't get to," Banks replied. "The chamber here's out, as we can hardly lock ourselves in."

"There's more ammo out on the hill, where we left it. I could take Wiggo and..."

"Nope. Too risky. And the colonel's orders are to sit tight and wait."

"So we wait."

"Aye. We wait. But not here. There are too many windows and doors to defend easily. We need one room, one entrance to funnel the fuckers towards if need be. Take Wiggo and do a reccy of this courtyard. Find us a spot we can defend without using all our ammo up at once."

Banks stood at the doorway with a knot in his stomach as Hynd and Wiggins left to circle the yard. Every time one or the other was out of sight inside a building, the knot tightened. Standing by watching men being put in danger on his orders never got any easier but the day it did, it would be the day he walked away from the life.

It took the two men ten minutes to check out the courtyard and on their return Banks knew from their faces that the search had been futile.

"There's a lot of dead bodies, cocooned like the ones down in the town by the river," Hynd said. "And not a defensible spot to be had…at least none any better than we've got here."

It made his decision an easy one.

"That settles it. We stay right where we are. And if they come for us, we fall back to the chamber, shut the door enough to keep them out, and then we wait for nightfall."

Hynd didn't say it but the question was clear in his face.

And then?

*

Once they got the heavy door open again, Banks had the others move all the gear back through to the mosaic chamber and ordered Davies to stand guard.

"Watch yon hole up in the corner, lad. Anything tries to come through, blow it to buggery."

Wiggins brought in the camp stove and coffeepot.

"And get a brew on, there's a good lad," Banks added.

Maggie had returned with Wiggins and was now sitting alongside the other woman with an arm around Kim's shoulders, neither of them speaking. Banks only got a nod of thanks when he passed 'round a smoke for her, Wiggins, and himself.

"Chin up," he said to her. "Just a few more hours."

Maggie didn't reply but it brought a sob from Kim, and led to a fresh burst of weeping.

"Let her cry," Banks said softly. "This is a good sign."

Maggie rose and walked with Banks when he returned to the main doorway. Once there, they smoked in silence for a while before she spoke.

"How do you cope with it?" she said. "The death, I mean. There's Kim, frazzled and strung out, catatonic, Reynolds and White gone, the rest of the team taking the mystery tour down river and me living on smoke, yet you and your men aren't affected."

"Oh, we're affected all right," Banks said. "I promise you that. But the training tells us to put that away while there's a job to be done. If it's not helping, it's not helpful. But believe me, we're affected. With me, it comes mostly on dark quiet nights, at three in the morning. That's when my dead come back to haunt me, that's when the training means bugger all."

"What helps?"

He showed her his cigarette.

"These and booze. Plenty of booze."

She must have seen the truth of it in his eyes, for she went quiet at that and when she finished her smoke she left without another word.

*

It remained quiet until around midday. Banks did his best to keep it that way, making sure the men rotated around at regular intervals to stop boredom leading to slackness. They drank coffee, smoked, and kept guard, watching the alleyways and rooftops.

For a while, Banks dared to hope that the firefight in the alleyway had been brutal enough to scare the beasts off from another attack. But after the sun passed its highest point and the shadows stretched across the courtyard, Banks caught a glimpse of movement on the rooftop directly opposite them. One of the dog-sized spiders crawled below a parapet, only its round back showing. Another followed in its wake, then more until there were a dozen or more gathered along a stretch of roof.

One finally showed itself, raising up half the body. A pair of front legs came up, waving, as if tasting the air. Banks studied the beast through his rifle sight, the first chance he'd been given to take time in studying their attackers. As a boy, he'd studied a variety of insects up close under both magnifying glass and microscope and this had the same look to it, of something too large to be real yet so fascinating he couldn't look away.

The front end looked oval, slightly flattened, with a pair of black, sharp fangs around the mouth, which was little more than a moist tube. He remembered from those childhood investigations that arachnids had no way of chewing food; they like to pierce with the fangs and suck at the juices. The fangs of this one dripped wetly with the same venom that had raged through White, and there was a cluster of a dozen red eyes sat above that, all of which stared back down the scope at him. As if it sensed it was being watched, the sharp fangs clattered together, the rat-tat-tat of its call echoing across the roofs, to be answered by a persistent drumbeat that came from all around, scores, perhaps hundreds of spiders, all calling out in unison.

Banks' mouth went dry as he lowered his weapon and shakily lit a fresh smoke.

They've got us surrounded. We're under siege.

- 12 -

Kim started talking around noon. At first, it was only to ask for water, then, as if a tap had been turned on in her throat, a torrent of words, about the dig, the mosaic, fragments of history about the city, worries about her parents and home and complaints of hunger. It came out as a long mixed-up stream.

"Are there any sandwiches? The Persians didn't have sandwiches. Oh, they had bread and they might have put meat or cheeses in it but it wasn't a sandwich. They broke the Roman's siege easily enough, I wonder where they got the stone to make the mosaic? Maybe they dug it out the ground and that's why there are so many tunnels. My mum will be worried sick."

There most obviously wasn't any mention of what had happened to Reynolds.

Maggie didn't push it and let her ramble. But something Kim said about the siege of the town when under Roman occupation got her thinking.

"Tunnels, you said?"

Kim perked up, as if eager to answer something that meant she didn't have to remember anything problematic.

"Yes. It's a warren under the town. And there is a multitude of storerooms and mine workings. The underpinnings of this place are supposedly riddled with them. It's how Shapur the First and the Persian army got in and ended the Roman era here. We haven't seen them yet. We can't leave without seeing them."

It wasn't archaeology that concerned Maggie; it was the thought of dark places, deep places, spaces where a horde of spiders might spin and sleep, contented for decades, centuries, until disturbed.

"Do you know how to access these tunnels and workings?" she asked.

"Nobody has been in them for more than a hundred years," Kim replied. "But on the last major expedition, there was an entrance discovered via the synagogue on the west-hand side of the main square. That's how the Victorian explorers got in and…"

Kim kept rambling, off in details of finds that now resided in museums across Europe, down to who had collected them, who had catalogued them, and where each piece could now be seen on display. It was an impressive feat of mental agility and one Maggie didn't know the woman had possessed until now.

But she's not talking about Reynolds.

Maggie knew that a voluble rush like this one would probably lead to a hard crash and sooner rather than later. She resolved that she would be close by when it happened. Kim was going to need a friend to get her up again.

*

When Kim finally stopped talking it came suddenly, mid-sentence, and Maggie was surprised to see that the other woman had fallen asleep sitting upright against the wall.

Wiggins had come off watch and was preparing a fresh pot of coffee. He looked over and smiled.

"Let her sleep," he said quietly. "It'll keep her from fretting."

Maggie pried herself carefully away from Kim and went over to where Wiggins sat, taking a smoke when he offered.

"How's things outside?" she asked.

"Much the same. They've let us know they're there, on the roofs. We watch them and they watch us and as long as neither of us makes a move, we're all happy that it stays that way."

"And what about when we need to make a move?"

"That's hours away yet. The captain will have a plan by then."

She heard the confidence in the statement.

"What's it like, to have that much faith in someone who holds your life in his hands?"

Wiggins laughed.

"We don't think about it like that. He's in charge, we do what he says, and we trust him to be right, more often than not. It's how the system works."

"It's not that I don't trust you," she replied. "But I've always taken care of myself and now I've got you lot looking out for me, I feel like a spare wheel around here. It's got me all itchy and worried and I'm not usually like this."

"Don't worry, lass. The cap's definitely right more often than not. He has got us out of some tight spots before. This might seem like a nightmare to you but I could tell you stories that would turn your hair white. It's who we are. It's what we do."

"But it's not all smooth talk and plain sailing, is it? You lose people too, right? Not everybody always makes it?" Now it was her turn to see that she'd struck a nerve as Wiggins' smile vanished and a heavy sadness showed in his eyes. "Sorry, I didn't mean that to sound harsh."

"No, you're okay, you weren't to know," Wiggins replied. "I lost a pal on the last mission. The wound's raw. But I meant what I said. The captain will die first rather than let harm come to you. So would I for that matter. As I said, it's what we do and why we do it."

*

When Wiggins left to ferry coffee to the others on watch, Maggie sat thinking about what he'd said. Davies was standing in the doorway, watching the hole in the high corner.

"Did you hear any of that?"

"Aye. And he's right. I'm new to the squad but I see the strength in the older lags. They signed up to serve. It was different for me. I just wanted to get out of Easterhouse."

"I don't blame you there," Maggie said, remembering the seedy, tired tower blocks she'd seen on a brief visit with an old boyfriend some years before.

She got a laugh in reply.

"God's own country, so they say. Skinny lads like me can get into all sorts of bother on a big estate like that, especially when they're seen as different, not really Scottish. I was constantly getting told to 'go back home' and I'm sure you know all the names I used to get. Being called Joshua didn't help much either, not in Glasgow. I don't have much of a family, there's only my old ma and me. So I became a Joe and found myself a home, made myself one. These lads here are my family. Trust the corporal. Trust the captain. Trust the squad. We'll get you back to your home."

Maggie took a long drag at her cigarette and waved it at the private.

"If the cancer sticks don't get me first. Getting me smoking again isn't doing much to keep me alive."

"I wouldn't be too sure," Davies replied, smiling. "It's giving you something to do, something else to think about. That's kind of the point and why so many of us do it."

*

After she finished the smoke and reminded herself not to take another one from any of the men for a while, she wanted some fresher air in her lungs so headed back out to the main doorway. The younger men, Brock and Wilkins, were watching the two rooms in the corridor, with the three officers, all of them smoking, standing at the main doorway at the entrance. She told Captain Banks what Kim had said about the tunnels.

He listened intently.

"So there might be a way out without going through the streets?"

"That wasn't what I was thinking," Maggie replied. "I was thinking more in the sense that there might be a spider lair down there."

"Aye, there's that too," Banks replied. "But an underground escape route might be exactly what we need later. Do either of you know how to get down there?"

"I think Kim does," she replied. "But whether she'll talk about it again is fifty-fifty at best. She's a bit shook up."

"We're all a bit strung out. Try to get some rest. When it comes time to go, we'll be moving fast."

Maggie motioned out over the courtyard.

"Anything going on?"

He pointed her to the rooftops, where for the first time she saw the rounded backs of spiders showing above the parapets.

"Two dozen at our best count. But no more of the big buggers like the one back in the alley."

"Maybe that was the only one?"

She saw in his eyes that he believed that as little as she did.

"Wiggins tells me you found a depiction of them, in a Roman mosaic?"

Maggie nodded and told Banks about the find. Again, he listened intently before replying.

"And it shows them coming out of a cave in the hill? More tunnels? The more I hear of this, the more I think it might be our best bet for a furtive exit. See if you can get Kim to tell us how we might manage it? Please?"

- 13 -

After the woman left the doorway, Banks sent Wiggins to check on the younger privates.

"See how they're holding up, Wiggo. And remind them to conserve ammo. No shooting unless I order it."

"Will do, Cap," Wiggins replied. "Do you think there's anything to yon story about tunnels? Could we slip away unnoticed?"

"Only if we're lucky. And that's not been working too well for us this trip so far."

"What we need is a fucking huge rolled up newspaper. The fuckers would never ken what hit them."

"Do you have one up your arse?" Hynd said. "No? Then stop talking bollocks and see to your men. The captain gave you an order. Fuck off and obey it, there's a good corporal."

Wiggins smiled and gave a sarcastic salute but left in a hurry.

The sarge lit another smoke from the butt of the last but Banks refused one when it was offered and went back to keeping a close watch on the roof. If Maggie was right and these things had a lair in underground tunnels, it didn't prevent them being out and about for long periods in blazing sunshine.

Which might mean the tunnels are our best bet. If the beasties are up here, they're not down in the dark.

The information had given something that had been in short supply in the past few hours: hope.

*

It remained quiet for another twenty minutes and Banks was starting to think they might make it through to dusk without a shooting match. Then he saw a shadow move out of the corner of his eye and turned, looking east across the courtyard. A spider as big as the one they'd killed in the alley to the north, a creature the size of a small car, climbed slowly down off the roof and began to weave a web across one of the three alley entrances off the yard.

His first instinct was to shoot it but he fought down the urge.

"Cap?" Hynd said quietly at his side. "Do we take the fucker out?"

"We can't afford to get into a firefight. It's too long until our pickup. If we provoke them and they decide to attack, we don't have the firepower to hold them off for long enough."

"And what if they cover all our escape routes with the buggering web?"

"Then we'll have to find another escape route," Banks replied. "But as long as it's spinning its pretty patterns, it's not over here trying to eat our faces. So we leave it be, let it get on with whatever the fuck it's doing."

"Setting a trap is what it's fucking doing," Hynd replied but didn't push it, merely went back to sucking at his cigarette.

Over the next hour, they watched as the huge spider filled all three of the visible alleyways with a thick tangle of webbing, gray walls that Banks knew from earlier experience could be cut through but not without a lot of hard work and time they might not have.

"Sarge," he said, thinking out loud. "Do you think that web stuff burns?"

"Well, I remember as a lad putting a lighter to a spider's nest in my auld granddad's hut and it went up like a rocket, so I'm thinking, aye, it'll burn."

"My thoughts too. We're going to need some fuel to get us out of here. Go tell Wiggo to stop making coffee. We have to conserve what's left in those wee gas tanks."

*

They swapped watch shifts mid-afternoon, with Wiggins and Brock taking the door, Wilkins and Davies watching the windows of the rooms inside, and Banks and Hynd taking the chance to get some hot field rations inside them in the main chamber.

Banks also took the opportunity for the first time to have a good look at the mosaic in the dug-out section of the floor. Seen anywhere else, it might have been taken as a remarkable feat of imagination but Banks had now seen the spiders and was pretty sure the artist responsible for the mosaic had been working from real life experience. The attention to detail was equally remarkable and despite it being worked in tiny pieces of polished stone, it was possible to make out fine details of weapons and armor on the soldiers attacking the spider in the center. But something else caught his attention, activity around the opening in the hillside that was the origin of the spiders.

"Can you map this against the current topography of the town?" he asked and Maggie rose from beside Kim to join him.

"Given how the skyline is depicted, we think the cave is outside the main wall, somewhere on the north side of the escarpment, facing the river. Why do you ask?"

He pointed at a group of three men, not armed but pouring something from barrels down into the cavern mouth.

"What's this, do you think?"

"Kim thought it might be hot oil, or maybe tar?"

"Aye, that's what it looks like to me too. There's nowt in the historical record about spiders, right?"

"Right."

"Which means these folk that made the mosaic succeeded in getting them under control, maybe even wiping them out for a while. It wasn't big beasties that drove the Roman's out, was it?"

"Nope, it was Persians, at least that's what everything in the historical record says."

"And these Persians didn't mention spiders either?"

"Not as far as we know."

"Then they can be stopped. And if the Romans could do it with the limited tech they had back then, I'm sure we can do even better."

He allowed himself a smile. He was starting to develop a plan.

*

Banks was pondering some ideas when his thought processes were interrupted by a shout from out in the hall. It came from Wilkins.

"Sir, you need to see this."

Banks followed the shout through to where Wilkins stood guard at the window.

The body of the dead man, White, had been propped, sitting in a corner of the smallest room several hours previously. Only now it wasn't so much a body as a collapsed sack of skin that looked to be held together only by the clothing. His head had dropped forward onto his chest, which was a blessing; given what the rest of him looked like, his face would have been too terrible to behold. From a not-too-close inspection, Banks believed that every bone in the man's body had turned liquid, remolding his internal structure to little more than an amorphous blob. He remembered the spider's sucking mouth and realized what they were built to suck. He had to fight down a sudden gag reflex.

That wasn't even the worst thing. The reason Banks didn't get too close was the stench, a sickly odor of corruption he knew too well from the aftermath of old battles. The smell came, not so much from the body but from a spreading pool of gray and green fluid, a puddle into which what was left of the body was slowly sinking.

"How long has it been like this?" Banks asked.

"The smell's been bad for a wee while, sir," young Wilkins said. "But I've been standing by the window and didn't pay that much attention until I turned round to see…that."

"Aye, well, it can't stay here, that's for sure."

He didn't notice that Maggie had come in behind him and was at his shoulder, her eyes wide with horror as she looked down at the body.

"We should take him home," she whispered. "His family…"

"…don't want to see him in this state. Trust me on that."

He looked down at the body again. The leaking fluids were definitely spreading and the smell was getting worse. He turned to Hynd.

"Sarge? We got any tarpaulin?"

"No can do, Cap."

Maggie whispered again, "We've got the rucksacks. We could…"

She couldn't finish the sentence. Banks could hardly blame her. The man had been her colleague, maybe even friend. Pouring his remains into a nylon rucksack wasn't something worth thinking about.

He put a hand on Maggie's shoulder.

"We'll deal with it," he said. "It comes with the job."

He looked over her shoulder and met Hynd's gaze. The sarge nodded and went to fetch the rucksacks.

*

In the end, they needed to use a spade from the dig and scooped the man's remains, like so much wet cement, into the bag of one of the rucksacks, sealing that as tight as they could, then tying the first rucksack inside the second. What had been a man was now a wet ball of skin and pus no larger than a football, wrapped inside two nylon bags. They kicked dust and sand over the puddle of fluid until the stench abated, although there was a malodorous whiff coming from the rucksacks.

They took the bundle out to the main doorway and set it against the wall outside.

"We should at least bury him," Maggie said, having followed them through.

"Cremation might be preferable," Banks said softly. "But I can't spare the fuel. If we get a chance, we'll do better by him, I promise."

"We can't leave him lying against the wall."

Wiggins spoke, quietly and softly, "Lassie, there is not him, not anymore. Your friend is gone."

The woman looked like she might argue but was given no time. Across the square, movement on the rooftops signaled that the impasse had been broken.

- 14 -

Maggie struggled to drag her gaze from the tied up bundle of rucksacks, finding it hard to come to terms with how quickly Jim White had gone and been reduced to this state. She only managed to look away when she noticed that the soldiers had become silent and alert.

She looked up and saw what had caught their attention; dog-sized spiders, a score of them, lined the rooftops. They all stood on their back legs, their front legs raised in the air, as if tasting the breeze.

"What are they doing?" Wiggins asked.

"Do I look like the fucking spider whisperer?" Hynd replied.

"I can make a good guess," Maggie added. "I think they can taste the decay. It was their venom that caused whatever happened to Jim. I think it's part of the feeding process."

A rat-a-tat clacking echoed around the courtyard as if in reply, all of the spiders in unison.

"They're hungry? That's what you're saying?" Wiggins replied.

"No," Banks replied. "She's saying we've got bait."

Maggie balked at that.

"That's not what I said. I won't let you use poor Jim as a fucking enticement."

"Sorry," Banks replied. "But he's a tactical advantage."

"Tactical fucking advantage? He's a human being."

"He was," Banks said.

And as quickly as it had come, all fight left her. The bald declaration of fact hit her hard and she remembered Wiggins' and Davies' words from earlier. White was gone and these soldiers were only looking for a way out of the current situation, a way to keep her and Kim alive. She needed to start helping rather than hindering them.

No time like the present.

"So what can we do now?" she asked.

The spiders stood in a row along the rooftops, tasting the air but showing no signs of venturing down from their high position.

"If they're happy to wait, I'm happy to oblige," Banks said.

A high scream echoed through the building from deep inside.

Shit, it's Kim. We left her alone.

*

Maggie was right behind Banks and Wiggins as they ran along the corridor and into the dig chamber, so she got a far too close look at the spider that was trying to force its way through the gap in the top corner where the walls met.

The only thing that had kept Kim alive was that this beast was too large to get through the hole and had only managed to get its mouth, eyes, and two legs into the room before getting itself stuck. It struggled, fangs clattering, caught in the gray webbing that had covered the hole. Pebbles and dust dropped from around it as it frantically tried to widen the gap enough to allow it through.

Wiggins raised his rifle, aiming for the cluster of eyes.

"Wait, Wiggo," Banks replied, putting a hand on the barrel and lowering the corporal's aim. "I want to try something. Fetch me one of the gas canisters we use for the stove."

The corporal left and returned a minute later. In the meantime, Maggie went to where Kim sat against the wall, her gaze fixed on the struggling beast in the corner. When Banks took the canister, open the valve, and set the escaping gas aflame with his lighter, Kim spoke up, shouting, her voice stronger than it had been for days.

"Burn it. Burn the fucker."

Banks turned to her and smiled.

"That's the general idea, miss."

He stepped forward, taking care to keep out of the way of the spider's mouth and applied the flame to the webbing around it. The result was spectacular. Fire flared, yellow and green and blue as the web went up with a whoosh. Banks had to stand back as a halo of flames encircled the beast. It thrashed and let out a high wailing squeal. Its struggling became frantic as it tried to back away from the flame, only to get more entangled in web, which itself then caught fire, encasing the whole gap in the wall in fire.

By the time the flames started to die down, the spider had stopped struggling. The front end of it caved in, a lump of ash and burnt carapace, only a dark hole left where the eyes had been, and finally there was only two badly charred legs hanging from the hole to show it had been there.

"That went well," Wiggins said.

*

"Thanks," Kim said to Banks.

The captain smiled again.

"Your idea. Or, your wee mural here's idea anyway," he said and looked at both Kim and Maggie. "You two are the smart people here. Why don't you put your heads together and see if you can come up with something else that might help us?"

Banks left, leaving Wiggins at the door to watch the gap in the wall. The hole looked wider than before, as if the spider's death throes had caused structural damage to the wall.

"What do you think is through there?" Maggie asked Kim. "You mentioned tunnels earlier."

"I did? I don't remember. But yes, the literature talks of tunnels, mine workings, perhaps even tombs from several different cultures."

Maggie stepped over to pick up one of the lights and took it over towards the gap.

"Careful, lass," Wiggins said from the door. "Don't get too close. Spiders are sneaky wee buggers."

"I want a wee look through there, that's all," she said. "Keep me covered."

She had to stand on tiptoe to see anything, then had to push the light through the gap at the full extent of her arm. She got a sight of a wall covered in ornate carvings, the paint on the rock looking fresh and vibrant although she knew it must have been hidden for centuries, perhaps millennia. The whole expanse of wall she could see was covered, ranks of carvings reaching to the limits of her light. When she called out, the echo from the new chamber beyond told her it was a much larger space than the room in which she stood.

"Kim, come and look," she said. "We've got a major find through here."

"Come away, lass," Wiggins said. "Find or not, there's no way you're going through there. It's not going to happen, so put the idea away."

"I'm an archaeologist," she said. "It's what I do."

"Aye, maybe. But you can't take it with us when we get out of here tonight. So let it be. You might get a chance to come back at a later date, when it's safer."

Maggie looked through to the new chamber again.

So close.

"Look, I'll only be a minute. I'll take a camera through, at least get it recorded. You can cover me from this side."

Wiggins shook his head.

"No can do, lass. The cap would have my balls for breakfast."

She smiled.

"Not even for a promise of a curry and a bottle of wine when we get home?"

He laughed.

"And I thought the spiders were sneaky buggers. Sorry. I'm in no hurry to get busted back to private on my first trip out. And that's what you'd be doing to me if you push it. Please. Don't."

"Then I'll see if I can appeal to your captain," she said and made for the door.

"Good luck with that," Wiggins said with a laugh. "He doesn't like curry."

- 15 -

"Nope," Banks said a few minutes later. Maggie had come to him with a tale of a new find that needed recording for posterity and she'd made a good case for herself but he couldn't allow it. It was too risky. "Wiggo was right to keep you out. For one, we already know there's spiders through there. It's too dangerous."

"The thought of new wonders never before seen, just out of reach, is something I'd never be able to live with. And besides, you said yourself you wanted intel about a possible escape route?"

"That was before I found out that fire works better than bullets against these buggers. We'll burn our way out of here through the alleys if we have to."

"Let me go through with Wiggins," Maggie said. "Two minutes, tops, and I promise I'll be careful. He can check for a possible way out, I take a few photies, and everybody gets what they want?"

Banks looked out over the courtyard, to where the exits were all closed off with thick web and to the black shapes lined up along the rooftops. The more he considered it, the more he thought that a backup plan was a good idea.

"Okay, then. But I won't send Wiggins through. I'll accompany you on your wee jaunt."

"Thank you," she replied and smiled. "Wiggins was going to cost me a curry anyway."

"In that case, you owe me a pizza," he replied. "Lead on."

*

Wiggins raised an eyebrow when he saw that Banks had yielded to the woman but wisely kept his mouth shut.

"I'll go first, you follow me, and Wiggo watches our backs," Banks said to Maggie. "And any time I say enough, it's enough and we get out of there. Understood?"

She looked up from where she'd been checking the batteries on a digital camera and gave him a mock salute.

"I should come too," Kim said but the other woman hadn't left her place sitting against the wall and Banks saw she'd said it but not meant it and a hint of relief showed in her face when he spoke.

"Nope. We're pushing our luck as it is. A quick in and out is what's needed here."

"So the sarge's wife tells me," Wiggins replied with a grin.

"Game head on, Wiggo," Banks replied. "Any eight-legged fucker shows up, put it down hard and fast."

Banks handed Wiggins his rifle, hauled himself up and through the gap, getting oily ash over his palms for his sins, and got his weapon back before dropping down into the other side. He kicked aside the dead body of the spider, then stood with his back to the wall, switched on his gun light, and washed its beam across the room. He saw why Maggie was so interested. The room was some twenty feet square and lined from floor to eight feet tall ceiling in large panels of stone-carved and painted frescos. They didn't look Roman. Banks was no archaeologist but these had a sense of an even greater age and if he had to hazard a guess, he might say Babylonian, given the epic beards on show in some of the carved men and the ancient weaponry on show in their hands. The spiders that were depicted in the carvings were the same though; large as chariots and emerging from holes in the ground to wreak havoc.

He was examining a scene of graphic dismemberment—men and spider—when Maggie pulled herself through to join him. She immediately set to taking pictures. He left her to it and stepped over to examine the only exit.

He knew before he reached the door that it was going to open into an even larger area beyond; he heard the echoes of his padded footsteps and felt a breeze on his face, cool and welcoming after the stifling heat out in the building through the hole.

More of the gray web hung around the door and when he shone his gun light out into the open area, there were steps leading down into a vast underground cavern. Web hung everywhere he looked, in thick mats across openings and stretched in cat's cradles like rope bridges over the rocky roof. But apart from the dead one he'd kicked out the way, there was no sign of current spider activity.

There was a definite drag mark leading down the steps and off into the gloom beyond his light and at first, he was at a loss to explain it. Then he remembered: Reynolds must have been taken this way. He decided not to mention it to the woman behind him, at least not until they got back to the other side. All he heard was the soft whistle of wind as if coming from a distance and the click of the camera as Maggie took picture after picture.

*

He knew something was coming before he heard it; there had been a subtle change in the breeze, a hint of acridity and a shifting of the air.

"Time to go," he said, taking Maggie by the arm and leading her towards the corner

"I'm nearly finished."

"No, you are finished."

Then they heard it, the now familiar rat-a-tat clacking of a spider, somewhere, not too far away, out in the larger chamber and definitely getting closer.

"Quickly now," he said. "Get out of here."

Maggie took several precious seconds to stow the camera safely away inside her shirt before scrambling up the wall to the hole, her feet not taking hold on stone that was slimy with the oily residue of dead spider. Banks had to turn away from the doorway to give her a boost, cupping a foot in his hands and lifting, hard, throwing her up through the gap in the wall.

The spider clacking was even louder now, right outside the doorway.

"Come on, cap," Wiggins shouted.

Banks knew that if his own foot slipped the same way that Maggie's had then he wouldn't escape an attack.

"Fetch that gas canister, Wiggo," he said. "Then cover me."

He turned his back to the wall, weapon raised, light shining on the doorway. The rat-a-tat clacking went up a notch, frenzied now, and a shadow, a large one, moved in the larger chamber outside the door.

"Cap?" Wiggins said above him and he looked up, saw the canister in the corporal's hand, and nodded.

"Drop it."

He caught it smoothly, then had to lower his rifle to get at his lighter. As if aware that the weapon was no longer trained on it, the spider came into view. It wasn't as large as the big ones he'd seen outside but it filled most of the doorway. It clacked its fangs together fast, as if in anticipation of an easy meal.

"Come and get it, fucker."

Banks opened the valve on the canister, stepped forward, flicking the Zippo open and rolling the wheel at the same time. It took immediately and he applied it to the gas, sending a sheet of flame washing over the spider. The flame also took hold on the web around the doorway, which flared up yellow and green as it burned and dripped, viscously, like napalm, onto the spider's body. The creature gave out one high squeal and retreated fast, patches of burning web stuck to it, still flaming.

Banks went to the doorway and saw the burning beast escape into the darkness. But the flames showed him something else; red eyes, reflecting yellow and green in the flames.

Scores of them.

*

If he'd turned and ran then, he knew he'd make an escape easily.

But that'll leave this lot at my back.

He had a better idea.

Avoiding the already diminishing flames, he stepped out of the doorway, down three of four steps.

"Cap?" he heard Wiggins shout, worriedly.

"Be back in a sec," he said.

The rat-a-tat clack of spiders in unison echoed around the chamber. They'd seen him and he heard the scratch of hooked feet on stone as they came forward.

He opened the valve of the canister to full, set the lighter flame to it, and threw the can into the largest mass of thick web he could reach. He was already turning back up the steps when it went up like a grenade at his back, sending a sheet of flame running all along the length of the chamber's roof, dripping blobs of melting, burning web on the spiders below. They thrashed and squealed in frenzy, their attempts to escape

84

only spreading more flame around. He waited long enough to see the flame take hold on the walls, then turned and ran for safety.

Banks was smiling as he let Wiggins help haul him up and out of the room.

*

Banks and Wiggins stood in the dig chamber, feeling a wave of hot air and an acrid tang in the air waft out from the hole, weapons ready should anything come their way. But all they got was the extra heat and smell and even that faded as the cooler breeze from earlier eventually reasserted itself.

"Was there a way out that way?" Wiggins asked.

"Hard to tell," Banks replied. "But there was definitely a way in for the beasties. So maybe aye, maybe no but at least we should have given them pause for thought about coming this way again for a while."

- 16 -

Maggie accepted another smoke from Wiggins after the captain left the room, satisfied nothing else was coming through the hole. She sat with Kim, perusing as well as they could the photos she'd managed to take in the chamber on the other side. Some were slightly blurred and out of focus and the small flash on the camera hadn't helped matters but she'd got enough clear images to show a good range of the painted carvings and more than enough to get Kim excited.

"Definitely Babylonian," Kim said. "And if I'm reading it right, they're all of the same period, from the reign of Hammurabi, which puts the work at 18th century BC, around when he conquered this area as part of his empire building. This is major league, Maggie, fortune and glory stuff. It's definitely the earliest find on this site and something no one has ever seen before. We could live for years off the research needed on this new room alone."

Maggie nodded in agreement.

"You should see it, Kim. The photos don't do it justice. It's vibrant and dazzling, like it was painted yesterday."

"We can only hope that fire didn't do permanent damage. It would be criminal negligence on our part if we found it only to fuck it up an hour later."

Wiggins spoke from the door.

"The fire was all outside in another area beyond and a wee bit around the doorway. There'll be a bit of smoke and maybe some ash, nothing that can't be wiped off with a damp cloth. Your paintings and carvings are all okay, or were when I got my last look."

"I hope so," Maggie said. "For I swear on my mother's grave, I'll be back someday, to make sure they're preserved properly." She echoed Wiggins' words of earlier back to him. "This is who I am. This is what I do."

As soon as she said it, she knew it for truth. Despite, or maybe even because of, what she'd seen and experienced here, she had resolved not to let it scare her off what was her duty, her reason for being here in the first place.

"And I'll be with you," Kim said, surprising her. The other woman had got over her earlier funk; Maggie guessed it was a combination of passing time, seeing the efficiency with which the soldiers had seen off any threat to them so far, and now a rising excitement at the implications of this new find.

"I mean it," Kim continued. "This is important, historically so. We can't walk away. I know I couldn't."

"Aye, well good luck with that, girls," Wiggins said at the door. "This place is a war zone and will be for years yet. I know you got in this time but after this clusterfuck here, I don't see anybody getting permission for a while. Besides, with these spiders about, it's probably safer to fuck off and nuke the site from orbit."

"It's the only way to be sure," Maggie said, smiling thinly to show she got the reference. "But I have the photos. When I show them to top people in the field, they'll be able to put the pressure on for the sending of a real relief team."

"As I said, good luck with that," Wiggins replied. "But if you ask for backup, make sure I'm on holiday at the time. I bloody hate spiders."

*

"Look," Kim said, looking up from the phone. "They're in groups,

10 rows of 6 to each. It's definitely early Babylonian. They did all their counting in sixties; it's why we've got 60 seconds to a minute, 60 minutes to an hour."

"A wee connection from them to us," Maggie said, looking over to Wiggins. "It's another part of why I do what I do; history isn't something that happens and gets forgotten. We connect to it, in wee ways, ways we'd only notice if they were gone." She motioned at the gap in the wall. "And that through there is a big bloody connection. We can't let it be lost."

"Hey, it's not me you've got to sell it to, lass. I'm only a lowly squaddie who goes where he's telt to go. And don't bother bugging the cap with it either. I can tell you now he'll sympathize but he can do fuck all once the brass have made up their minds. Our job here is to get you home. So that's what I'm going to do; I can at least make sure you get yon photies in front of somebody who might actually give a shit."

*

Maggie spent a few minutes taking more photos, of the mosaic in the dig this time, making sure she catalogued it fully. It was while she was taking a close up of the depiction of the cave on the hillside that another thought struck her.

"The tunnels you mentioned earlier weren't as old as this new find, were they?" she asked Kim.

"No. The ones I was talking about were built during the siege, when the Persians were trying to tunnel in and the Romans were trying to hold them at bay. The last big dig here, in 2009, found 20 dead men in one near the north wall and there was bitumen and sulfur coating the bodies. There's another connection to the present, for that was a chemical warfare attack, with the Persians pumping gas into tunnels and suffocating the defending forces. The latest theory is that's how the siege was broken"

Wiggins stopped her and spoke to Maggie.

"Go tell that to the cap," he said. "I think he'll be interested."

*

"This tar and sulfur," Banks said five minutes later after she'd relayed the info. "Do you know where it is? Have you seen any deposits?"

"No to both questions," Maggie replied. "But Kim said it's by the North Gate."

"So it might as well be on the moon, for all the good it is to us here," Banks replied. "But all intel is good intel, so thanks for that."

They stood at the main doorway and Maggie was glad that Banks blocked her view to where the rucksack sat against the wall outside. She saw that the shadows had lengthened considerably since her last look out, now covering the whole of the courtyard save for a small triangular patch in one corner. Up on the roofs, the rounded humps of the spider's backs showed on the skyline.

Banks saw her looking.

"They've lost interest. There's been no movement for an hour or more. It's a Mexican standoff, for now. But it'll be dusk soon enough and I'm going to have to break the deadlock without getting us all killed if we want to get out of here."

Maggie looked to where thick webbing covered the alleyways that were their exits from the courtyard. She saw the problem.

"Even if you burned the mass of web there, the spiders could drop on us from above."

"Aye. And there's no guarantee that there's not a shitload more web beyond that. We'd be caught in a tight funnel, under pressure of numbers, with too little ammo for a prolonged firefight. That's one of my problems. I've been considering a sneak getaway through the tunnels beyond your new find. But we already know that's also spider territory and again it'll probably be a tight space. I'm not sure which option gives us the best chance of getting away free."

"If I get a vote, I say try the tunnels," she replied. "I never liked finding a spider in my hair."

- 17 -

The spiders blinked first. Banks was on guard at the main door with Private Wilkins when the beasts made their move. The first sign of activity was a pair of legs reaching up to be silhouetted against the sky, then dragging a bulbous body up onto the parapet. The spider raised its front end and its fangs clacked out a rapid message that echoed long and loud around the courtyard. It was obviously a sign, a call to action, for within seconds several dozen of the dog-sized beasts had joined the first on the edge the roof.

"If they come, save your ammo, lad," Banks said to Wilkins. "If you can't put it down with one shot, don't bother. And if they don't stop after we get a few of them, we'll fall back to the back chamber. We need to make sure we've got enough ammo to get us to the chopper when it comes."

It looked like the spiders were intent on pressing their numbers advantage. All of the ones visible on the skyline began a slow, steady descent of the walls, heading for the courtyard below.

Wilkins' face had drained of all color, his eyes wide and a bead of sweat running down the bridge of his nose.

"Steady, lad," Banks said. "They're only beasties. It's not as if they'll be shooting back at us. We've got the firepower advantage for the present. Keep them at a distance."

The first one hit the ground and immediately scuttled forward, multiple red eyes fixed on their doorway. Banks waited until he was sure of his target and put a single shot into the middle of the red eye, blowing most of the front of the spider away in the process and sending the thing, now only a tangle of frantically waving legs, crashing to the ground.

Wilkins' first shot missed his target, as did his second. By that time, a dozen of the spiders were heading at speed across the courtyard towards their position. Banks put another one of the down with a well-aimed shot then, seeing that Wilkins' marksmanship clearly wasn't up to the target practice required, pulled the lad back into the hallway.

"Back up, slowly," he said. "We're pulling back to a better position."

He got on the headset to Hynd.

"Sarge, we're coming in. All fall back to the chamber. But save ammo where you can. We're going to need it later."

He was only able to watch as three of the spiders broke away from the main pack and took note of the remains of White in the rucksack. They tore at the material in frenzy, like starving dogs after scraps, throwing fragments of nylon far and wide across the courtyard and sucking greedily at the spilled contents. Soon there was nothing remaining of White but a damp puddle on the ground and even that was already drying out in the residual heat of the day.

Hynd buzzed Banks' headset.

"Come on back, Cap. We've got you covered."

"We'll be right there."

Then there was no time for more talk. The approaching spiders were too close. He had to retreat, keeping himself between the spiders and Wilkins as the creatures massed in the doorway. He was able to pick off two more of them with shots to the eyes when the attack hesitated at the doorway but all his shots did was spur the rest of the spiders into action and they came on fast. He had to expend more ammo than he'd hoped to keep them at bay, even when they reached the first room in the corridor and Brock and Davies joined them in covering fire for the retreat.

They were at the second doorway and the door to the chamber opposite when more spiders scuttled in through the first room that Brock had vacated. Hynd stood at the second doorway, weapon ready, but couldn't fire for fear of hitting the rest of them. The spiders swarmed, filling the corridor floor to ceiling, climbing over and around each other in their thirst to get at the men, the rat-a-tat clacking of their excitement as loud as the soldiers' weapons.

There wasn't time to get them all back to safety and get the door closed before the spiders washed over them. Banks knew it would deplete their ammo far too quickly but he had no choice but to give the order.

"Rapid fire. Take these fuckers out."

*

The sound of them all firing at once was deafening in the confines of the corridor. Casings flew, the air filled with thin smoke, and dazzling muzzle flashes lit up the walls like a rock concert strobe. Bits of spider leg, body, shell, and internal fluids splashed as high as the ceiling and pooled on the floor and the noise was a deafening drum of thunder. It only lasted ten seconds but it felt like an eternity before Banks called a halt.

"Cease fire. We got the buggers."

The corridor rang and echoed with their shots for a few seconds, then everything fell still as they looked across an expanse of torn remains of the dead beasts. Then they heard it, coming from out at the main doorway, a new, incessant rat-a-tat, sounding angry now, a chorus of spider talk, getting closer fast. A fresh attack was imminent.

"Right, that's enough fucking about. Fall back," Banks said. "Into the chamber and shut the door and make it fast."

He stayed in the corridor until the last second, covering their rear while the squad filtered into the chamber. Wiggins and Brock put their shoulders to the door, inching it closed with a loud rasp and creak of stone on stone. It was nearly shut when Banks saw three more spiders appear at the far end of the corridor, already coming for him over the remains of their dead.

He let off a quick volley of three shots, then squeezed inside, helping with his weight to close the door fully. It slammed into place, shearing off a single spider leg that had appeared in the gap. It fell to the ground quivering until Wiggins ground it to bits under his heel.

"Have I told you how much I fucking hate spiders?"

*

"Well this is nice," Kim said. "Back to square one."

"Not quite," Banks replied. "We've made a dent in their numbers if nothing else."

He turned to Hynd.

"Another inventory please, Sarge. I want to know to the exact bullet how low we're running. And get these gas canisters together. They might end up as our last line of defense."

The scritch-scratch of spider feet on stone sounded from outside the door.

"No offence, Captain," Kim said, "but I've been in this situation already. It's lost its appeal for me."

"And for me," Banks replied, "but I don't intend to stay around to experience it for any longer. We're going out that way."

He motioned to the gap in the wall. Maggie spoke up.

"You've made up your mind?"

The scratching got louder outside in the hallway and Banks smiled thinly.

"It's not as if we've got much choice. I'll go first, with Brock and Davies. Maggie, you and Kim in the center and the others will bring up the rear. We only move as a unit and we get out of the town the first chance we get. It'll be dusk soon enough and yon chopper will be waiting for our call, and might not wait if we don't, so we have to move fast and quiet. Are we all clear?"

Nobody argued.

He swung his rifle over his shoulder, stepped over to the gap in the wall, and hauled himself up and through to the other side.

- 18 -

Maggie went first after the three soldiers to show Kim how easy it was and waited on the far side to help the other woman through. Kim gasped aloud when she saw a piece of the rock carvings that were illuminated by the light on Davies' weapon.

"God, it's beautiful."

Maggie could only agree but they didn't have time to stop and look, for Wiggins was already coming through the gap above them.

"Move over, ladies," he said. "You wouldn't want me falling on top of you. Though I might enjoy it."

"You should be so lucky," Maggie replied and moved away quickly, leading Kim with her towards the doorway, where Captain Banks already stood, shining his light out into the chamber beyond.

"Looks clear," he said. He waited until Hynd and Wilkins came through, then went ahead down the steps out of the chamber. Maggie felt Kim's hand find hers in the gloom, she gave it a squeeze that she hoped was reassuring, then followed the gun lights out into the wider cavern.

*

The place stank, an acrid taste akin to burnt rubber and fine gray ash coated the floor, crisp as fresh snow on a cold day underfoot. Black scars on the walls showed where the burning had been at its most severe. The air felt stiflingly warm, as if the rocks had retained heat and were still radiating it. As they followed Banks, Maggie had an eye open for any more carvings and fresh find of significance but this chamber looked to be mostly a natural cavern in the hill with little sign of any working beyond the steps and doorway they'd just left.

Banks and the two privates, Davies and Brock, led the group directly up the center of the space, heading for a darker opening that could be seen to the north. They all soon had to step gingerly through the burnt remains of spiders, twenty at least of them, lying in heaps of ash and burned legs tangled willy-nilly together in their death throes. The smell was worse here, harsh in the nose and tickling at the back of the throat when she switched to mouth breathing. Despite holding a hand over her lips and trying to breathe shallowly, Maggie had to fight off a gag reflex. It got even worse when an incautious step meant her foot went down and into, the main body of a large spider, releasing a moist farting sound and an assault of acridity that choked her. She moved on quickly, fighting off an urge to scrape her shoe clean on the leg of her trousers, for that would only ensure the stench stayed with her all the longer.

Fortunately, the dead spiders were all concentrated in one area toward the center of the chamber. In the space of half a dozen quick steps, they were able to move through and past them, to join Banks and the two privates as they reached the shadowed exit at the north end. A welcome breeze came from the passageway ahead, colder air, mostly clear of the stench of burning and Maggie took a grateful lungful as the captain called them all together into a huddle.

"That was the easy bit," he said, keeping his voice low. "The earlier burning cleared the way for us. If we're lucky, the buggers have fucked off completely. But we can't count on that. We don't know what's ahead of us, so stay close, don't stray, and no shooting unless I order it. Sarge? Pass me one of the gas canisters. I'll take point. And if I say run, don't hang about. Understood?"

Everybody assented and Banks led the way into the dark opening.

*

The passageway narrowed quickly inside the entrance, so much so that after a dozen steps they had to move single file, although Kim would not let go of her grip on Maggie's hand. Maggie led her, like mother leading child, forward in the gloom, following the light of Bank's gun light ahead. After ten more paces, they came to a flight of worn stone steps, leading steeply downward. Banks stopped them again and they grouped tight in single file at the top of the stairwell.

"Bugger. I'd hoped to be going up into the city, not down into the hill. If anybody sees a passageway that feels fresher, shout. And if this one goes down too far, or if there are spiders ahead of us, be prepared to turn back fast. This is no place to make a stand."

Without another word, he led them down.

Maggie had to take care with her footing, for although the gun lights illuminated the way ahead, she could barely see her ankles in the dark when she looked down. Fortunately, the steps were dry and worn enough by feet over the centuries that her feet naturally found the grooves and ruts that made descending simpler. She tripped at one point and put a hand out to steady herself, surprised to find the rock cool, cold to the touch.

The going was of necessity slower now, for they were all taking care despite the relatively easy going; none of them wanted to take a tumble down into the black depths. The only sound was the pad of their feet on stone and their breathing. The whole descent took on an air of anticipation, Maggie's fight or flight response kicking in hard at the thought of what might be waiting ahead for them. If there had been any sudden loud sound, she might well have screamed; she certainly felt ready for it.

But Banks' fears of going too far down into the hill proved unfounded as they only went down twenty steps before the passageway opened out again into another chamber. Given the echoes raised ahead of her, Maggie guessed that this one was of similar size to the one at the top of the stairs. Banks waved his light around and once again Kim gasped loudly.

This was a natural chamber, or rather, it had been at one time. The squad's gun lights showed her enough to see that it had been worked into a long alleyway with evenly spaced eight feet tall cells hewn into the rock. Each cell was guarded by twin, intricately carved, pillars and each, at least the ones not covered liberally in spider web, contained hefty primitive double-stacked sarcophagi, four to a cell. They weren't close enough to make out detail but even from the bottom of the steps, Maggie could tell that these were Roman period pieces, of similar age to the mosaic they'd found on the floor in their dig. More than that, they looked like they had lain here undisturbed since being put in place, with only the spiders for company.

"Do you see this?" Kim whispered, as if unsure whether she was awake or dreaming.

"I see it," Maggie replied. "I'm not sure I believe it."

Banks called for quiet. He had his gun light pointed straight ahead down the center of the room, trying to penetrate the darkness. From what Maggie could see, the rows of cells continued away into the distance in a long alley. Banks motioned that Davies should keep an eye left and for Brock to cover the right, then led them, slowly, forward.

*

The breeze was stronger here, cooler too, and Maggie felt it brush hair against her ears. She hardly noticed, for after a few steps she remembered she had her camera. She took as many pictures of the cells and sarcophagi as the wavering gun lights would allow to her, trying different levels of zoom. She knew the light was too dim to do the scene justice and that many of her attempts would be out of focus or too dark to be of any use.

But I have to at least try.

Around half of the cells had their entrances covered with the thick gray mats of web she was starting to come to hate but none of the stone coffins looked to have been disturbed in any way. Maggie couldn't help but wonder what marvels they were walking past so blithely, what wonders had lay hidden in the stone all these long centuries. A find like this, undisturbed, was unprecedented, and in normal circumstances would mean years of meticulous work in her immediate future.

But these aren't normal circumstances.

She knew there was no chance of convincing Banks to stop to let her and Kim investigate. His priorities were to get them out and home and they were priorities she agreed with for the most part. All she could do for now was record as much as was possible with the camera and hope against hope to be able to return. Her vow to make that return trip was only strengthened.

"We should…" Kim started but Maggie stopped her.

"I know. But first we have to survive long enough to get home and tell somebody." She held up the camera. "At least we'll have this to show them."

"It's not enough."

"It'll have to be," she said.

*

The alley of cells ran for a hundred paces, heading straight north. As they approached the far end, they noted that all of the openings were covered in web. Maggie also saw that Banks had become even more still and alert ahead of them and decided it was time to stop taking pictures and paying more attention to her own immediate safety. She stowed the camera back inside her shirt, felt Kim take her hand again and, concentrating only on the gun light ahead of them, stepped forward behind the three soldiers.

The alley led to another doorway at the far end and more steps, leading upward this time, a short run of six that brought them up into another chamber with three doorways off, to the north, east, and west. This room was empty save for a single four-foot-tall sculpture in the center, done in white marble of a naked man wearing only a peaked cap, standing tall and wielding a spear that was pointed down at the body of a large dead bull. It looked to be complete, with no cracks, no chips, no bits of anatomy missing from man or bull. Maggie knew that any museum in the world would pay a king's ransom to have it among their exhibits.

"It's Mithras," Kim whispered. "God, that's beautiful. There's one in Paris that I've seen but this is in much better condition."

"Who's Mithras when he's at home?" Wiggins said behind them.

"An eastern sun god the Romans, the soldiers in particular, took for their own. Statues to him have been found in forts and temples all over the empire. Men like you have been worshipping him for millennia."

Wiggins laughed.

"Honey, there are no other men like me."

Banks hushed their chat again and looked to Kim.

"You've seen maps of this place. Maggie tells me there's an exit leading above ground in the synagogue. Any clue how we'd get there from here?"

Kim looked thoughtful, as if calculating directions and distances in her head.

"We must be under it if I've got it clear in my head," she said, then pointed at the rightmost entrance. "That way is my best guess. If I'm right, it goes up toward the square and the old synagogue is at the western end."

Banks looked to the north passage.

"The wind is coming that way though and I was inclined to follow it. But anything that gets us out will be good by me at this point. Davies, lead the way and look sharp."

*

A narrow, winding corridor led upward at a gentle slope from the Mithras room and after only a few minutes brought them into another, much smaller, room. The walls were rough-hewn and solid and it felt tight and cramped when all eight of them were inside. At first, it looked like a dead end. Then Banks spoke.

"Kill your lights," he said. The soldiers all obeyed and Maggie realized she could see their faces. Banks pointed upward and they all raised their heads, to look up what might at one time have been a chimney. Dim light came from a hole open to the sky five yards above them.

"Just as well it's not yet full dusk or we might never have noticed," Banks said. "Who fancies a climb?"

- 19 -

Banks was tempted to try the climb himself but as the officer in charge, he had a duty to all of them, not just to himself, and he was relieved when Wilkins, the smaller of the privates, spoke up.

"I'll give it a go, sir," the lad said, passing his rifle to Davies. "I always liked a good clamber."

They had to boost Wilkins up onto Davies' and Brock's shoulders before he could reach up into the chimney and when the lad pulled himself up, it was a tight squeeze. His body now blocked out most of the aperture at the top, so Hynd switched on his gun light and tried to give the younger man some light for the climb. Wilkins put a foot on the surface ahead of him, his other foot on the wall behind, and then began to shuffle himself upward in a classic narrow space climb.

It was slow going and Banks knew how much strain the lad was putting on his ankles with every move. About halfway up, Wilkins paused to catch his breath.

"It's going to be tight," he called down, "but I should get up there okay."

Banks was already thinking it wasn't a great idea, for if Wilkins, the slightest of them, found it tight, the broader lads like Brock and Wiggins would have no chance of making it. He was about to call Wilkins back when the lad started climbing again, making better time now. Banks let him continue.

At least he'll get us some intel as to where the fuck we are.

Wilkins reached the top some minutes later.

"Nearly there," he called down.

"Don't do anything daft, lad," Banks called up. "But see if you can get some pointers as to where we are."

They heard a scrape as Wilkins pushed himself up.

"There's a big market square here. We're in the south-west corner by the look of it and...oh fuck." There was more scrambling above and Wilkins dropped down the chimney, far faster than he had gone up. "Spiders, sir," he said as he landed, unsteady on his feet beside them. "It's infested. Fucking hundreds of them and at least a dozen of yon huge buggers the size of cars.

"That settles that then," Banks said. "We go back to the room with the statue and try north."

Kim spoke up.

"If we're in the southwest corner of the square, we must be close to the synagogue."

Banks smiled grimly.

"And if the square is infested with spiders, there's not much point in going that way or even looking for that exit. We don't have the ammo for a prolonged firefight, so it's best if we sneak along unnoticed for now. If we manage to maintain a track north, we'll hit the outer wall at some point. You said that's how the Persians got in?"

Kim nodded.

"But that was many centuries ago."

"It doesn't matter. If the way is blocked and we need an explosion, I'll get Wiggins to fart."

He looked up the chimney. It was already appreciably darker up there. Dusk was coming on fast.

*

When they arrived back at the Mithras statue, Banks took the lead again and led them north, feeling the cool breeze on his face. It gave him hope that he was doing the right thing, although the lack of a backup escape route had him worried; if they met the spiders in these enclosed corridors, they'd be able to hold them off for a few minutes, then it would be all over. The need for a clear escape was uppermost in his mind and he walked ahead as fast as he could while allowing the others to keep up at his back.

The corridor here was worked stone rather than rough rock and that too gave him hope that they might be emerging into a different area of tunneling that might yield better exit points.

He had his rifle in one hand and one of the gas canisters in the other. Having seen the carnage fire could wreak on the spiders and their webs, he had more confidence in that than he had in bullets, although he knew he'd need precious seconds to open the valve and get a lighter to it. The rifle was his backup for that contingency and he kept the light pointing straight ahead as he went quickly along the corridor.

It wasn't long before he came up hard against another dead end, although this one wasn't even a room; the corridor simply came to an end at a stone wall with only a small square opening covered in an iron grate at eye height ahead of him. It was a little more than a foot square.

The others came up close at his back as he shone his light through the grate. It showed another, large, chamber beyond and the breeze was strong at his face as he peered through.

He dropped his rifle to his side on its strap, pocketed the gas canister, and put both hands on the iron bars of the grate, pulling with all his strength. It moved, only slightly but enough to give him hope.

"Back up, give me room," he said as the others crowded around him. "Sarge, Brock, watch our backs. Wiggo, get up here and give me a hand. We're going through here, one way or another."

It took several minutes of hard graft but finally the grate began to slide out of its moorings and one last hard tug broke it free completely. They dropped it to the floor at their feet, where it clanged and echoed, ringing like a loud bell in the enclosed space.

Something answered in reply, the rat-a-tat chatter of spiders calling out in unison from somewhere behind them.

*

"Right, Wiggo, you're up first. Get your arse through there and cover us, we've got trouble inbound," Banks said. "Davies, follow him through, then Maggie and Kim. The rest of you watch that corridor. They won't be able to come all at once, there's not enough room. That's all we've got going for us."

Wiggins went first through the new hole, scrambling head first, pulling his rear end through with half an inch to spare.

"Good," Banks said. "If your lardy arse gets through there, the rest of us will have no trouble."

Davies went through fluidly and athletically in comparison to Wiggins' scrambling, as did Kim after him. Banks was thinking they were going to get away safely when the sarge spoke at his back.

"We've got incoming, Cap," Hynd said. "Fifteen yards and closing."

Banks boosted Maggie up and through the hole before turning to look down the corridor. Several sets of red eyes reflected back from the gloom. He retrieved the gas canister from one pocket, his lighter from another, and stepped forward between the other men and the spiders.

"Wilkins, get through to the other side. Sarge, Brock, cover me."

"What the fuck do you think you're doing, Cap," Hynd said.

"Buying us time," he said and walked forward towards the spiders.

*

He smelled them before he got a good look at them, the acrid and bitter odor stinging in his nostrils. Four sets of red compound eyes looked back at him as he closed the distance. For every two steps forward he took, they took one toward him and soon there were only a few paces between him and the spiders. Moving slowly, he opened the valve on the gas. The spiders chattered at that but didn't react until he flicked on the lighter, the click-clack of the Zippo too loud, like gunfire in the corridor. It elicited another rat-a-tat response.

One of the spiders proved to be bolder than the others and scuttled quickly forward. Banks stepped up to meet it, applied the flame to the escaping gas, and sent a wash of fire over the thing's head, which took light immediately. The beast, already burning hard, tried to flee backward. Banks stepped in closer, feeling heat singe his eyebrows and tighten the skin at his cheeks as he sent more flame washing, over the thing's back this time. It continued to flee from the fire, running directly into the other spiders, which also burned.

Banks dropped the canister as the gas exhausted itself, swung his rifle into his hands, and sent bursts of three shots each into the bodies, which collapsed in ash and flame. The corridor at this end filled fast with acrid smoke, the stench even worse than previously, but the job was done; none of the spiders moved and fire was eating them fast, leaving little but oily ash in its wake.

He turned to head back to the others. Wilkins was most of the way through the hole, with Hynd waiting to go next. Brock had Banks covered, his gun light showing the way back to safety. He had only got halfway back to them when he saw from Brock's face that they'd got trouble.

Then he heard it, a louder clacking than ever. He looked over his shoulder to see a huge spider scuttle over the burning embers of the others and barrel down the corridor at speed, coming straight for him. It was so large its body touched each wall and its eyes looked like a small throbbing mass of fiery eggs, fixed directly on him.

It came so fast he wasn't going to have time to turn, aim, and shoot, and he knew he was blocking Brock's line of sight. He took the only option open to him. He rolled forward, turning and dropping to the floor, his weapon raised, as the spider loomed over him. He put three shots into its belly before it fell on him, knocking all breath out of his body. His ears rang as three more shots followed—Brock, he guessed—then three more as Hynd joined in. He felt wet, gore running over him from the holes in the beast, which now felt a dead weight above him.

Then the weight was gone and Brock and Hynd stood over him, having rolled the dead thing away.

"Do me a favor, Cap," Hynd said, helping him to his feet. "Save the heroics for when the colonel can see them. They don't do my auld ticker any good."

Hynd helped him back to the hole in the wall and boosted him up.

"Get through there before you do yourself, or us, any more mischief...sir."

He went headfirst, halfway through when he heard Brock call out from behind.

"Here they come again."

*

Banks squirmed through the hole, helped by Wiggins pulling from the other side, then immediately stood and turned, aiming his rifle through the gap, adding his light to Brock and Hynd's. It reflected off half a dozen compound eyes at the far end of the corridor. The loud rat-a-tat clacking meant there were more spiders piled up further back in the darkness.

"Sarge, get through here, that's an order. On the double."

He had to step away to allow the sergeant to come through, so he didn't see what happened next but he could make a good guess; the spiders had noted that Brock was exposed and launched an attack. The sound of Brock's return fire came loud even through the blocked hole.

Hynd fell head first out of the hole and both Banks and Wiggins stepped forward in unison, their weapons raised. Brock stood with his back to them, firing into a wall of spiders that crawled along the floor, the walls, and even the roof in a squirming mass of thick bodies and hairy legs.

"Get down, lad," Banks called and Brock went to his knees while the three of them pumped round after round into the approaching spiders. They put down the front rank quickly enough but more quickly moved forward to fill the space. It was the situation Banks had feared; a mass attack in a confined area. They were lucky to have got their people out through the hole.

But that doesn't help Brock.

"I'm out," Brock shouted, dropping his rifle and reaching for his handgun. Banks knew it wouldn't be long before he too ran dry.

The spiders kept coming.

*

"I'm dry," Wiggins said and stepped back. Davies filled the space quickly barely missing a beat in the firing. Spider bodies littered the corridor floor, reaching to Brock's feet now. Banks knew he was down to his last few rounds and was about to step out when he felt warmth near his ear.

"Fire in the hole," Hynd shouted and Banks ducked as a flaming gas canister soared past his head and through the hole, halfway along the length of the corridor. Brock, thankfully, had the good sense to duck and cover, and Banks looked away as the small tank went up in a roar of flame that set spiders running and scurrying off into the dark distance along the corridor.

Banks wasted no time.

"Private Brock, get through here, right now."

Brock scrambled into the hole and began inching his way forward. Banks immediately saw he'd been wrong earlier; Brock's rear end was the equal of Wiggins', if not even larger, and the private was having trouble getting through.

"For fuck's sake, man, get through here. Remind me to put you on a diet when we get back."

He and Wiggins took an arm each and began to pull. They'd almost got Brock all the way through when he let out a yelp of pain. They tugged harder and he popped out like a cork out of a bottle. The front end of a large spider filled the hole where he'd been. Fangs the length of fingers clacked excitedly together.

Hynd stepped forward and put three shots in its eyes. It fell away from them, giving them a sight of a vision from hell—the whole corridor beyond was filled with a mass of squirming, scuttling spiders. Some of them smoldered, some of them were burning and spreading more flame as they tried in vain to find escape. Hynd had a remedy for that too. He lit another canister, stepped forward, and casually dropped it through to the other side of the hole.

"Duck," he said, smiling.

- 20 -

The torrent of noise, flame, and confusion were too much for Maggie's senses to bear. She stood to one side of the hole in the wall, holding Kim's hand while the fighting raged. The noise only faded after the sergeant dropped the canister through to the other side. It went up with a flash and a soft whump. Flame came back through the hole, accompanied by high, wild shrieking from the other side.

Then everything fell mercifully quiet.

The silence was only broken seconds later by Brock. The young private had sat down, slumped against the wall.

"Sir, I think I'm in trouble."

Maggie was first to bend to him and her heart sank when she saw the deep slashing wound at the man's ankle. It was already starting to blacken at the edges.

Just like Jim White.

Private Davies pulled her gently aside and went to work on the wound but all Maggie could think of was how quickly it had taken White and how much he'd suffered.

Captain Banks stood looking back through the hole, from which black smoke drifted slowly to hang above them.

"All clear, for now," he said. "Sarge, get the ammo redistributed. I want everybody to at least have a few rounds available in case of emergencies."

Hynd moved to comply and Banks turned to Davies.

"How's the lad?"

"It's a deep one, sir. I got some peroxide in it straight away and I'll bandage him up good. He's going to need something for the pain and we'll need to keep an eye on him until we get him to a real doctor but he should be okay to move out, as long as we don't have to do any running,"

"Jim White went out like a light within minutes," Maggie said.

"Toxic shock, probably," Davies said. "I'm hoping getting the peroxide on it early will prevent that."

"Aye, and I'll have some of yon high-class drugs, please, doc," Brock said through gritted teeth. "It's like somebody's pressing a red-hot poker against my skin. I'm hurting bad here."

*

While Davies administered to his new patient, Maggie had her first chance to look around this latest chamber they'd arrived in. She could only see what the gun lights showed her but it was obviously another room that had been extensively carved, although these had none of the vibrant paint colors they'd seen earlier. She got Wiggins to train his light on a particular patch that looked more intricate than the rest.

Kim pointed at the distinctive, simple outline depicting a basic carving of a small fish.

"Jewish. 1st century at a guess," she said. "Hebrew inscriptions, Early Christian imagery. And if I'm reading this right, it's a depiction of Paul's conversion on the road to Damascus. This is more than important, it's historically significant. The find of the century."

"Fortune and glory, Indiana Jones shite?" Wiggins said and Kim smiled thinly.

"Why, Corporal, do you have a whip?"

"Ask me nicely," Wiggins replied with a grin of his own until Banks put a stop to the banter with a sharp glance that shut the corporal up fast.

Maggie took more pictures while the opportunity was there but it was only a matter of seconds before Banks announced they had to move.

"I have to catalog this," Maggie said.

"If it doesn't help us get out of here, it's hindering," Banks replied. "You'll get to come back, if you help me keep you alive for a wee while."

She dragged herself, reluctantly, away from the carvings and followed behind Banks and Davies, heading out an entrance to the north of the chamber. Kim took her hand tightly again. Brock hadn't fallen victim to the coma that had taken White and limped along, helped by Wiggins at his shoulder, with Wilkins and Hynd bringing up the rear.

*

They arrived immediately in another archaeological wonder, a set of chambered catacombs, obviously, to Maggie's eyes, of the same Jewish period but the ravages of time and looting had not been kind here. Broken sarcophagi lay tumbled along the walls, fragments of skeletons and clothing showing where looters had desecrated the tombs in search of anything of value.

"Bastards," Kim said.

Banks spoke from the front of the group.

"This is a good sign," he said. "We've reached areas where people have been relatively recently. Keep an eye open; if looters can get in here, we can get out."

At least the area was free of any webbing and they were able to progress for thirty paces along the center of the catacomb chamber. As they closed on the far end, Maggie saw two exits ahead of them, both little more than darker shadows in the gloom.

"Right goes toward town, left goes toward the outer walls, is that right?" Banks asked.

Both Maggie and Kim replied at the same time.

"Yes."

Maggie continued, "But there's no guarantee either way and..."

Banks put up a hand to stop her.

"I know," he said. "But we already ken that the town is infested, so we can't realistically go that way. I'm hoping there's some way out for us to get to open ground where the chopper can reach us easily. It's about the only plan I've got, unless you've got anything better?"

Maggie had no answer to that. Kim held her hand tighter as they went left, into a narrower corridor of roughly hewn rock that sloped gently downward.

*

It was only a few steps inside before Maggie noticed a smell in the breeze, a vinegary tang. There had been so many noxious smells assaulting her nose and throat in the past hour that it took her a while to identify this new one but once she noticed it, there was no mistaking it.

"There's spiders around here somewhere."

"No shit, Sherlock?" Wiggins said at her back but Banks took note and stopped at the front.

"Yes," he said. "I smell them too. But what choice do we have?"

He turned back and continued onward. After only a dozen more paces, the corridor opened out into another worked area, an empty, cathedral-like space of pillars and arches that was more recent than anything else they'd seen so far. Half a dozen opening led off to the left and right and they could see, right at the edge of the gun lights, a darker, larger opening leading out at the far end to the north. Fresher air came from that direction and Banks led them toward it, upping his pace.

"Late Persian. 4th century," Kim said. "A storeroom at a guess."

It was a fine feat of architecture but there were no carvings, no statues and Maggie took some pictures where the light allowed it, more to document their trail than from any archaeological curiosity as they made their way through the large, empty area. It was while she was taking one more photograph that the relative quiet was shattered by a loud rat-a-tat clattering from behind that was immediately joined by others, coming from openings both to the left and right.

Banks broke into a run and they all followed.

*

When they reached the exit at the far end of the chamber, they found it was a wide and high archway, leading into a man-made tunnel of expertly worked stone, eight feet in circumference. Banks stood aside to let Maggie, Kim, Wiggins, and the injured Brock in behind him. The other four soldiers stood in a line at the entrance, waiting for an attack.

None came, although the clattering rat-a-tat echoed from all the other exits and when Banks swung his aim at the nearest to the left, it showed two sets of the red compound eyes reflecting back at them.

"It's as if they want us to go this way," Maggie whispered.

"Aye," Banks replied. "We're being herded, like so many bloody sheep."

She didn't ask what they might be being herded toward.

I don't think I want to know the answer.

- 21 -

Banks stood under the archway for several seconds, weapon trained on the exit off to his left, but the eyes of the spiders merely gazed implacably back at him, the beasts showing no sign of pressing an attack, content merely to block off the exits.

The sense of being herded got even stronger when Banks turned away and once again led the group down the worked tunnel. Hynd spoke in his helmet after twenty yards.

"They're following us, Cap. Staying beyond our light. Should I let them have a volley?"

"Negative. Save your ammo. I've got a feeling we're going to need every bullet before too long."

The excited clacking of the spiders echoed around them as they went down farther into the tunnel. It descended in a gradual slope but there was little danger of falling as the path was dry and even underfoot. All they had to worry about was the spiders, which matched their pace, coming on at their back.

All of Banks' instincts were telling him they were heading into trouble but he'd brought them all this far and at each stage had made what he'd thought to be the correct decision for their safety. He could only hope he'd get a chance to make another.

*

He was starting to worry about the descent—it had taken a turn westward and was surely taking them under rather than toward the town walls. Judging distances in his head, he was pretty sure they were at the outskirts of town already and going deeper into the hill hadn't been on his agenda. But there were only spiders and death at their backs, so he kept them on their course.

They arrived at the foot of the slope when the tunnel opened out into a far larger cavern beyond where they stood on a rocky ledge. There was evidence here that there had been a cave-in and recently at that, for rubble and dirt lay strewn around the cavern and high above, some thirty yards up a rocky slope to their left, the last of the daylight showed at an open hole. It was the dim light that had caught Banks' eye first, so he was only alerted to the rest when Wiggins spoke, too loudly, at his back.

"Fuck me."

Banks dropped his gaze from the daylight above and took in the rest of the chamber.

It was as large and high-vaulted as a medieval cathedral but instead of stained glass and tapestries, this one was decorated in web, in traceries and rope bridges, vast flowing sheets as smooth as silk, and nets as geometrically perfect as any fisherman's. And right in the center, some thirty yards below where the squad stood on a ledge, in the center of all the webbing, sat a spider from out of an arachnophobe's worst nightmare.

It was all white, as white as the webbing in which it sat, the only color in it the deep, blood-red of the huge set of compound eyes and the twin jet-black fangs, each as long as a man's leg. The thing's legs, each more than fifteen feet long on their own, sat splayed on the web, monitoring the vibrations, while the bulk of the body lay in darkness beyond, a swollen, bulbous, fleshy thing, rounded like a globe and pulsing obscenely, as if ready to burst. The spider wasn't paying them any attention; all of its effort was going into feeding, as it plucked a human-sized cocoon from a pile in front of it, put it to its mouth and sucked like a child with a drinking straw, an obscene sound that echoed around the cavern.

"Where's Sigourney fucking Weaver when we need her?" Wiggins said at Banks' back.

Now that Banks' eyesight had adjusted to the light in the cavern, he saw that there were numerous other caves leading off down below them, passages from which the dog-sized spiders scurried to and fro. He realized with dismay what kept them so busy. They were retrieving football-sized white balls from the rear of the large spider and ferrying them off in their scores down into lower levels of the system.

Those are eggs. Hundreds of eggs.

He turned to Hynd and spoke softly.

"How many of those wee gas canisters do we have, Sarge?"

"Two, Cap. Want them?"

"Not yet. If we start a fire now, we'll fry ourselves into the bargain." He pointed up the rocky slope to where the light, fading fast to darkness, had come in.

"There's our way out. We head up there, double time, and if we get a chance, take this big fucker out from up there. We have to stay alive long enough to get above ground. I can call in the chopper once we're clear."

As a plan, it had the benefit of simplicity. But he'd forgotten about Brock's injury.

"I'm not sure Badger can make it up yon slope, Cap," Wiggins said.

"I'm fine," Brock replied but his skin had taken on a pale, greasy look and his eyes were sunk deep in their sockets. Every movement caused him a flare of pain.

"We'll fucking carry him if we have to," Banks replied. "But we're going up and we're going now before we get noticed."

*

Getting off the ledge proved to be the first hurdle to cross. The access to the slope and their way out was eight feet below their current position and no easy way to get to it.

"Sarge, Wilkins, watch our backs," Banks said. "We're going to have to take this as a relay."

Davies, as the tallest of them, went first, lowering himself off the edge then dropping lightly to his feet on a large slab of rock below.

"It's stable, sir," he said. "Send them down."

Banks helped Wiggins drop Brock down next. Davies managed to take the weight off the other private's bad ankle but Brock let out a yelp of pain on landing. The white spider paused in its feeding and its left front leg trembled, testing the web, but Banks was able to let out a slow breath when it went back to its feeding.

"Best hurry, Cap," Hynd said. "We're going to have company. Yon wee ones are coming up behind us in the tunnel."

Wiggins went next, dropping down beside Davies. Brock wasn't able to put his weight on the wounded ankle and could only sit on the edge of the rock while Banks lowered first Kim, then Maggie, to the waiting men.

"Time's up, Cap," Hynd said. "Here they come."

The remaining three men all dropped at the same time. The slab of rock moved, tilting alarmingly and sending a tumble of loosened debris deeper into the cavern. This time it definitely got the white spider's attention. It ceased feeding and looked up, the plate-sized red eyes directed straight at them.

"Move out," Banks said. "Up that slope, right now. The sarge and I will cover you. Shift your arses."

The first of the smaller spiders looked over the ledge above them as Wiggins led the others away as fast as the hobbling Brock would allow.

*

"I think we've lost the element of surprise, Cap," Hynd said evenly as two more of the dog-sized beasts appeared at the ledge above their heads. The only thing stopping them attacking was the presence of an overhang that, momentarily at least, had them confused.

"Time for the gas?" Hynd added, waving towards the main mass of web. "It's not like we're short of fuel."

"Not yet," Banks said. "We need to give the others a chance to at least get some way up the slope. How much ammo do you have?"

"Half a mag and a clip in the pistol."

"Same here," Banks replied. "Let's see how many of these buggers we can take down with the rifles. Save the pistols if we can and back off as slow as we can. We only make a run for it if that big white fucker looks like coming our way; we'd need a fucking cannon to make a dent in that."

The six others were already down off the slab of rock and had made their way to the foot of the rocky slope. Brock was clearly struggling, some paces behind the others and was about to tackle the incline when Wilkins dropped back to lend him a shoulder.

Above Banks and Hynd, the first of the smaller spiders made a tentative attempt to negotiate the overhang, before losing its footing and falling, a thrashing tangle of legs, at Banks' feet. He put a single bullet in its eyes and crushed its body under his heel.

The sound of the shot rang around the chamber and brought an answering rat-a-tat clacking from the white spider, three beats that echoed as loud as the gunfire and brought an immediate response. Spiders, varying in size from the small, dog-sized up to the ones as big as cattle or bigger, poured out of the cavern entrances on the far side of their queen and, as if coordinated by some invisible signal, came on at speed, heading straight for Banks and Hynd.

- 22 -

The shooting started before Maggie and the others were a quarter of the way up the slope. It was hard going, rock and loose pebbles underfoot, and they often slid back a step for every two they took upward. Brock and Wilkins were lagging ever farther behind, Brock being unable to put any weight on his bad ankle, which meant the two of them were negotiating the slope like a team in a three-legged race and with little success in prospect.

Below them, only now reaching the bottom of the slope, Banks and Hynd fought a rearguard action against a growing army of spiders, taking them out a single shot at a time, then backing away before finding another target.

Wiggins turned to Davies.

"Get the women up top and make sure it's all clear," he said. "I'll give Wilkins a hand with Brock and hang back to back up Cap and Sarge."

"Bugger that women and children first shite, Wiggo," Maggie said. "You know I can handle a pistol. Hand it over and I'll do my bit. Joe can take Kim if she wants to go."

Kim took Maggie's hand again.

"As you said, bugger that for a game of soldiers. I'm staying."

"God save me from mouthy women," Wiggins said with a wide grin. He took his pistol and handed it to Maggie.

"I know," she said before he could say anything and gave him her best Glasgow accent. "Aim the pointy end at the fuckers and keep firing until they bugger off."

Wiggins grinned again.

"My sisters are going to love you."

He left her standing with Kim and Davies and went back five steps down the slope to where Wilkins and Brock struggled over a patch of loose pebbles.

"Miss?" Davies said.

"You'd better start calling me Maggie, or there'll be trouble," she said. "And I've got a gun now."

It was Davies' turn to grin.

"I was going to say, we'll wait for those three to catch us up, then we make a push for the top."

"What about your captain and sergeant?" Kim asked.

Davies pointed down the slope.

"They'll be fine."

Maggie wasn't so sure of that but the two men were alive and backing away slowly from an advancing swarm of spiders. The smaller ones had become more cautious, coming forward more slowly now in the face of the rifles. But that had only served to give the larger, cattle-sized beasts time in which to come up out of the caverns and join the attack. The nearest of them was only ten paces below the two men and coming on fast. The sergeant took it out with a shot in its eyes but two more immediately scuttled into the vacated space and the two men had to retreat to avoid being overrun.

*

It took Wiggins and Wilkins another minute to get Brock up to where Maggie stood with the others. The wounded private was clearly struggling, his face gray and lined with pain at every step. Davies had them put the man down on a rock and Wiggins and Wilkins took guard while Davies bent to look at the ankle.

Maggie saw it was bad, but worse than that, she smelled it was bad. The bandages, fresh not that many minutes ago, were soaked through with stinking black and green fluid and black necrosis showed in his flesh both above and below the extent of the bandage. Brock's eyes fluttered and he struggled for breath.

"I'm done," he said. "I can't go any farther. Go on without me, I'll cover for the captain and sarge."

"Don't talk shite, lad," Wiggins said. "You got this far, didn't you? On your feet, Private. That's an order."

To his credit, Brock made the attempt and got halfway up before his leg gave way beneath him but that brought a fresh flare of pain and a yell from him that echoed around the chamber even above the gunfire from below. It also brought another wash of stench from his venom-soaked bandages.

Maggie wasn't the only one to take note. The giant white spider lifted up its front legs, tasting the air in the same manner as she'd seen the smaller ones do outside when they caught a whiff of poor Jim White's remains.

Three of the large spiders in the forefront of the attack at the foot of the slope also mimicked the giant's response.

They think he's food.

Brock looked up at Wiggins.

"Thanks for looking after me, Corp," he said. "Tell my maw I went out fighting."

He looked up at Maggie and winked.

"Bait, eh? That sounds like a plan to me."

Before any of them could move to stop him, Brock rolled away to his right, sending himself tumbling in a flurry of loose rock, dirt and pebbles, not down towards the captain and sergeant but off to one side, heading directly toward a large mass of web.

"Badger, get the fuck back here, that's an order," Wiggins shouted but the private was already thirty, forty yards away, tumbling and rolling. By this time, Banks and Hynd were in full retreat and catching up to their position fast. A large number of the spiders broke off from the hunt, front legs raised and tasting, before turning and making directly towards where Brock had finally come to a halt, stuck tight in a fibrous mass of web.

Luckily for him, he had his arms free and got his pistol out in time to put two spiders down that were almost on him.

*

Wiggins was yelling profanities when Banks and Hynd arrived at their position.

"What the fuck happened?" Hynd asked as Banks put two shots into a large spider. It fell backward and took four more with it as it rolled away in a tumble of rock and rubble, buying them precious seconds of respite.

"Badger's playing the fucking doomed hero," Wiggins replied.

They all looked down the slope and saw Brock fumble in his jacket. The flare of yellow and orange as he flicked on a lighter showed as a bright spark in the gloom.

A mass of scuttling spiders encroached on his position. His yell of defiance carried clearly up the slope.

"Come and get it, fuckers."

Brock applied his lighter to the web below him.

- 23 -

Banks saw what was about to happen in his mind's eye even as the flames took hold and Brock burned.

"Run," he shouted. "This place is going up."

Without needing to be ordered, Wiggins and Wilkins, as two of the men with the most ammo remaining, covered the rearguard action while Davies hurried Maggie and Kim on at the front. Banks and Hynd, both now reduced to their handguns, were in the middle doing what they could to both run and pick off any of the attack that the two men behind them couldn't handle. What firing they were doing was limited to an occasional swivel, turn, and shoot, for the bulk of their attention was on running; the fire in the cavern had quickly turned into a conflagration.

The white giant thrashed and clacked its fangs like gunshots as molten, flaming web dripped down from the roof and spattered across its body, staring new fires in the web around it. The huge bulk of its body quivered and it thrust itself out of the space it had been inhabiting, making for the slope, either hoping for escape upward, or attempting to seek revenge on the squad. It hardly mattered which, for if the beast reached them before they reached the top, it would be game over for all of them.

Banks was already feeling the strain of the climb at calves and ankles and his breath came heavier at the exertion. The white spider and a large entourage of others of various sizes, were advancing fast, coming up and out of what was now a wall of flame below them. Waves of scorching heat washed up from below, fanning the flames in the cavern to greater intensity and Banks saw that it was now spreading over the roof. If it burned above them, they'd have the napalm-like drips to worry about as well as the spiders.

"Sarge, we'll need that gas," he said.

Hynd took one canister for himself and Banks took the other.

"Do we light them?" Hynd asked.

"No, lob them down towards the fire. Once they heat up enough, they'll go up like Roman candles. The delay might buy us enough time to get up top."

They tossed the canisters in unison, lobbing them high over the heads of the two men at the rear and down towards the spiders to land in front of where the giant was leading its troops upward. Both cans came to a stop outside the range of the flames.

There was no time to stand and wait to see if the flames would engulf the gas canisters; the pack of spiders, too many to be held back, scuttled towards them. Many of the beasts were burning and flames licked at the rear of the mass of them, taking heavy toll of their numbers. The rat-a-tat clack of a chorus of fangs echoed loud above the gunfire.

The squad fled upward, as fast as they could manage.

*

The canisters went up as Davies and the women reached the opening at the top of the slope. One of the small tanks blew directly underneath the giant white, blowing a huge, burning hole in its belly that spread quickly to engulf the whole beast. Its death throes screeching rang around the chamber like nails on a chalkboard. The second canister took out a dozen of the smaller beasts and two of the horse-sized ones and set more flames dancing around what few patches of web were not already burning.

The heat had become stifling, every breath a searing hot pull of pain in Banks' chest. Only the sight of the opening and Davies and the women waiting for them at the top of the slope kept his aching legs pumping. Wiggins and Wilkins were now running alongside them, both men having expended their rifle ammo in the retreat.

Spiders snapped and clacked at their heels and the first drops of molten, burning web began to spatter around them from the ceiling high above.

They arrived at the top ahead of a wall of flame falling from the roof in a fiery waterfall and threw themselves out of the chamber and upward into fresher, cooler air.

*

There was no time for rest. Heat came up behind them as if they stood in front of an open furnace door and spiders, some burning, were right at their backs.

The opening led, not outside into the open ground as he'd hoped, but into the inside of a ruined tower. A wall of rubble blocked any quick escape out onto the escarpment and the only immediate retreat available was up an internal flight of stairs against one of the tower walls.

"Up," Banks yelled, pushing Davies ahead of him. "It's our only chance."

The staircase was narrow. Davies went up first, Maggie and Kim hard on his heels, Wiggins next, then Wilkins, with Hynd, then Banks at the rear. The nearest spider, one of the dog-sized ones, was on him as he reached the bottom step. He used his rifle like a club, swinging the stock hard against the beast's body, sending it sailing away to tumble downward. The opening below him was already filling with a mass of burning spiders, all attempting to flee the flames at their back, only a few of them paying attention to the escaping squad.

One of the larger, cattle-sized ones took note of Banks' position and came forward onto the steps after him. He tried to use the rifle to club it like the last one but this beast was onto the trick and caught the weapon fast between its fangs. A tug of war ensued, one that threatened to pull Banks off the stairs and back down into the thronging spiders below. He let the spider have the weapon and, in the same movement, drew his pistol and put a single shot into its eyes. It fell, a dead weight, down onto the stairs at his feet, providing a barrier that served as a blockage to allow him to retreat faster upward and he was half a dozen steps higher before the dead beast got tugged aside by three of the smaller ones. They all stared directly at Banks as they came up the stairs behind him. He retreated, firing.

By the time he reached the top of the flight and joined the others on top of the tower, he'd nearly emptied the clip of the pistol.

More spiders kept coming up the stairwell.

*

He expected the others to have come up with a plan of escape but found them all standing on top of an open tower, looking out over the escarpment. He saw why they hadn't descended when he looked down.

It was full dark now but the carpet of stars and the red glow from fires provided more than enough light to see by. Several vents on the hill billowed out smoke and flame even as spiders came up out of them; hundreds, thousands of spiders, a mass of them covering the whole of the hillside. They varied from the dog-sized ones, to the cattle-sized ones and several that looked to be the size of small houses.

- 24 -

Maggie went to Davies' side when he stepped forward to cover the stairwell; he was the only one of the squad with ammo remaining in his rifle and she had Wiggins' pistol. The scene down the stairs was one from hell, a fiery conflagration in which spiders scurried up and over and around each other in frenzy to try to reach the stairwell and safety. There were some of the smaller ones on the stairs, coming up. Davies let them close in, hoping for a clear shot.

Maggie heard Banks at her back, on the satellite phone.

"We need an evac and we need it fast."

She didn't hear what was said at the other end but heard his reply clear enough.

"Two minutes. Got it. Come in on my signal, I'll leave the line open."

She had a glance over the small parapet, all that stood between then and the horde of spiders out on the hill. The beasts weren't paying attention to them at the moment but if that changed and they attacked, two minutes was going to seem a hell of a long time.

*

Davies took out the nearest two spiders with clean shots into the eyes. There was already one of the much larger ones at their back, pressing forward, a thing larger than a bull, fangs clacking angrily as it scurried upward at a full run, knocking the smaller ones aside in its rush, sending them down, shrieking, into the flames.

Davies put two shots in it but missed the eyes and it kept coming.

Maggie braced herself in a two-handed stance, fighting the tremble that threatened to spoil her aim. She took a deep breath and put two quick shots right into the center of the cluster of red eyes. The shock sent pain through her wrists and the crack of the weapon deafened her but she looked down to see the beast fall backwards into the fiery pit below.

Their shots had done more than deafen her. They'd caught the attention of the spiders out on the plain. Tens of thousands of red eyes turned as one and stared up at the tower.

Excited rat-a-tat clacking echoed across the night sky above the escarpment.

- 25 -

"Here they come," Wiggins shouted. They had two walls and a stairwell to defend and only Davies with any real firepower. Wiggins took his handgun from Maggie.

"No offense, lass, but I think I can do more damage with it."

Banks set Wilkins to watch the stairwell, had the women stand in the center of the tower away from the parapet, then put Wiggins and Hynd on the north side while he and Davies took the west, where the bulk of the spiders swarmed.

"Don't shoot unless they start climbing," he shouted. "And pick your targets. The chopper is inbound, any time now. We need to survive the next minute."

Even as he said it, they heard a distant thump of rotors.

"Lights coming in over the river, Cap," Hynd shouted.

"Okay, everybody, get ready to move, this is going to be tight."

He got on the sat phone.

"Good to see you guys. I hope you're packing. We need a strafing run before you come for us."

"Rebels?"

"Something a bit more exotic," Banks said, then had to put the phone in his pocket. Two large spiders scrambled up the wall directly below his position, scuttling upward as if defying gravity.

*

Davies sent the first of the two spiders back to the ground but needed three shots to do it. Banks put three into the other, right over the eyes, and it too fell away but when another took its place and began to climb, he pulled the trigger of his handgun and came up empty. Wilkins stood above the stairwell, surrounded by smoke and blasts of heat rising from below, firing down the steps. On the other wall, Hynd and Wiggins fired calmly and steadily downward and kept the beasts at bay. But it was a matter of seconds before they'd all be out of ammo.

The chopper came to their aid, cavalry riding over the hill at the last minute. It arrived over the north cliff of the escarpment and the pilot must have taken in the situation quickly, for he flew the length of the hillside, twin guns blazing, blowing a swathe of spider parts, legs, and gore into the air in a ten-meter-wide road.

"Yippee Ki-Yay, motherfuckers," Wiggins shouted.

They weren't out of trouble though, for a dozen or more of the smaller spiders were coming up the wall below Banks and Davies and Davies was struggling to hold them at bay.

"I'm out," Hynd shouted.

The rat-a-tat clacking of the spiders was louder even than their firing or the roar of the chopper as more began to climb.

*

The chopper came down on top of them, hovering less than six feet above, the downdraft almost knocking them off their feet until they found their balance in the roar of wind and sound. Banks motioned for Hynd to give him a hand and between them they boosted first Kim, then Maggie up into the arms of a waiting airman.

The squad fell back under the chopper as they boosted Wilkins up inside. Davies took guard while Wiggins went next, then Hynd leapt up, grabbed the door with both hands, and hauled himself aboard.

"Last call, lad," Banks shouted. "All aboard who's going aboard."

Davies threw his rifle for Banks to catch then leapt, more easily than Hynd had managed, catching the waiting arms of Wiggins above and being hauled up into the chopper.

Three spiders came over the parapet at the same time, giving Banks no option but to strafe them in a burst of fire that emptied the weapon but did the job of blowing the spiders to shreds and sending the pieces tumbling away below. He turned to make his leap for safety and looked up to see Wiggins' eyes go wide.

"Jump, Cap, jump now," Wiggins screamed, "that's a fucking order."

He dropped the rifle and leaped. Wiggins caught his left hand and for a terrible second he swung, one-handed, then almost fell when he felt a weight tug at his left foot. The chopper was already rising when he looked down to see one of the horse-sized spiders, clinging onto his boot by its fangs. He swung up, made sure Wiggins grabbed his free hand, then kicked out with his right foot at the beast's eyes, feeling something give, something soft, then the weight was gone. He looked down between his feet to see the spider fall back onto the top of the tower, a tower that was already completely overrun by scuttling spiders.

- 26 -

Maggie's heart was in her mouth right up until Wiggins dragged the captain aboard and only then did she start to believe that they might have made their escape. She saw Banks check around his foot.

"I'll need a new pair of boots," he said. "But it didn't penetrate, thank fuck."

The captain went up front and she saw him talking to the pilot and pointing at the tower below them. She went forward herself and looked out the window. The whole hillside swarmed with the spiders and they crawled freely all over the walls and turrets of the old town.

Banks turned to her.

"You're not going to like this," he said grimly. "But I'm not doing it for you. I'm doing it for Brock and for the members of your team we couldn't save and for all the folks in that town down river."

Maggie saw that the pilot's hand was over a firing mechanism.

"I think we can do a wee bit better than tar and sulfur," Banks said.

She looked in his eyes and nodded, echoing Kim's words from earlier that day.

"Burn them all. Burn the fuckers."

The pilot pressed the button and two missiles sped out, trailing flame in the night, diving down into the tower, the first taking out the tower itself, the second disappearing into the depths below. Two seconds later, fresh gouts of flame flared up out of the vents in the hillside, then the whole escarpment, spiders, towers, and the bulk of the old town fell away in on itself into the white spider's chamber. A wall of dust and smoke rose up, meaning that the chopper had to move away fast. After it banked and turned to bring the escarpment into view again, the smoke was already clearing.

The whole hill was now no more than a smoking crater, where nothing moved.

"I'm sorry," Banks said.

Maggie patted at where the camera sat inside her shirt.

"Don't be. I have the evidence. I'll be back."

She looked down at the crater one last time before the chopper turned away and they lost sight of it.

"I'll be back," she repeated. "I like to dig. It's what I do."

The End

CHECK OUT OTHER GREAT
CRYPTID NOVELS

BIGFOOT WAR
by **Eric S. Brown**

Now a feature film from Origin Releasing. For the first time ever, all three core books of the Bigfoot War series have been collected into a single tome of Sasquatch Apocalypse horror. Remastered and reedited this book chronicles the original war between man and beast from the initial battles in Babblecreek through the apocalypse to the wastelands of a dark future world where Sasquatch reigns supreme and mankind struggles to survive. If you think you've experienced Bigfoot Horror before, think again. Bigfoot War sets the bar for the genre and will leave you praying that you never have to go into the woods again.

CRYPTID ZOO
by **Gerry Griffiths**

As a child, rare and unusual animals, especially cryptid creatures, always fascinated Carter Wilde.

Now that he's an eccentric billionaire and runs the largest conglomerate of high-tech companies all over the world, he can finally achieve his wildest dream of building the most incredible theme park ever conceived on the planet...CRYPTID ZOO.

Even though there have been apparent problems with the project, Wilde still decides to send some of his marketing employees and their families on a forced vacation to assess the theme park in preparation for Opening Day.

Nick Wells and his family are some of those chosen and are about to embark on what will become the most terror-filled weekend of their lives—praying they survive.

STEP RIGHT UP AND GET YOUR FREE PASS...

TO CRYPTID ZOO

CHECK OUT OTHER GREAT CRYPTID NOVELS

SWAMP MONSTER MASSACRE
by Hunter Shea

The swamp belongs to them. Humans are only prey. Deep in the overgrown swamps of Florida, where humans rarely dare to enter, lives a race of creatures long thought to be only the stuff of legend. They walk upright but are stronger, taller and more brutal than any man. And when a small boat of tourists, held captive by a fleeing criminal, accidentally kills one of the swamp dwellers' young, the creatures are filled with a terrifyingly human emotion—a merciless lust for vengeance that will paint the trees red with blood.

TERROR MOUNTAIN
by Gerry Griffiths

When Marcus Pike inherits his grandfather's farm and moves his family out to the country, he has no idea there's an unholy terror running rampant about the mountainous farming community. Sheriff Avery Anderson has seen the heinous carnage and the mutilated bodies. He's also seen the giant footprints left in the snow—Bigfoot tracks. Meanwhile, Cole Wagner, and his wife, Kate, are prospecting their gold claim farther up the valley, unaware of the impending dangers lurking in the woods as an early winter storm sets in. Soon the snowy countryside will run red with blood on TERROR MOUNTAIN.

Made in United States
Orlando, FL
16 March 2023